BLACK CARD

BLACK CARD

A NOVEL

CHRIS L. TERRY

CATAPULT
NEW YORK

Published by Catapult
catapult.co

First Catapult printing: 2019

ISBN: 978-1-948226-26-4

Jacket design by Zoe Norvell
Book design by Wah-Ming Chang

Catapult titles are distributed to the trade by
Publishers Group West
Phone: 866-400-5351

Library of Congress Control Number: 2018965036

Printed in the United States of America
10 9 8 7 6 5 4 3 2 1

BLACK CARD

PROLOGUE

FALL 1997

I was finally black again. I sat on my bed, waiting for proof. Gray smoke oozed under my bedroom door and through the crack where windowpane met frame. The popping of needle on vinyl started so loud that I rubbed my thumb across my fingertips, expecting to clench the sound. A grimy hip-hop beat kicked in, with distorted drums, bass that rolled a pencil across my desk, and a half-measure loop of a soul singer wailing.

I steeled myself against the hurricane, pushing toes against floor, elbows against knees as I leaned in and bobbed my head short but loose, striking that tenth-grade balance of icy cool outside and whirring inside. I jumped when Lucius kicked the bedroom door open. His baggy jeans made a flag-in-the-wind snap as he stomped his boot. A black hoodie covered the top half of his face, but not his sparse goatee or the zit under his right cheekbone. I watched in silence, averting an identity crisis with every word I didn't say, every gesture I didn't make.

The door slammed shut behind him and he stepped to the middle of the small room, a husky specter floating in the sickly light. He jabbed his chin at me and I stood to face him, thumbs in my hoodie's kangaroo pocket, shoulders and head back, equally ghoulish.

"You had a big day, bruh," he said, his voice deep and rough for a teenager, cutting through the hip-hop beat.

I nodded.

"Let's see the highlights." He stepped to my right and pointed at the closed door. A beam of light shot through the opening between my curtains and a countdown flickered above the doorknob, 4-3-2-1. Lucius crossed his arms and we stood side-by-side on the scuffed floorboards, watching the makeshift screen.

Part one

Black-and-white footage of me in a polyester PE uniform, standing on a gleaming wood floor. My eyes widen in surprise when a basketball lands in my hands, then I seem to push it away. The camera follows the ball's arc across the paint and through the net. Quick pan back to my face shifting into a sunny grin as I hit a three-part handshake with another kid and hustle off-camera.

"A'ight," Lucius said. "You was lucky to hit that shot, but the daps at the end sealed the deal. I'm glad we been practicing."

I nodded and said, "Me, too," then kept my head moving with the beat. We turned back to the door.

Part two

A montage of me standing at my school bus stop with a slim backpack slung from one shoulder, slouching at a desk in class, and sprawling alone on my grandparents' couch, watching TV. In each shot, my eyes sparkle, my nose wrinkles, and I bring the top of my right fist to my mouth like I'm rocking an invisible microphone.

"Now that's the way to laugh," said Lucius. "We don't cheese. They don't need to see our teeth. This ain't a slave auction."

I did a purse-lipped smile, then flipped my hood up over my head, too.

Part three

Me on my bed an hour before, cradling a phone on my shoulder. The music in the room quiets to forefront the staticky voice of one of my old friends up north whining, "I can't understand you! Did you just say you wanted to *ax* me something?"

"Mmm-hmm." Lucius ran his eyes over my pale freckled face and kinky red-brown hair. "Your mixed ass might not really look like us, but the least you can do is try and sound like us."

I smiled again, agreeing silently.

Lucius punched my shoulder, then we repeated the handshake I did in PE, finishing by bumping chests to fists. Lucius stood back. The music cut out and the light grew angelic and bright. I sat on the bed as he swelled his chest and spoke with the gravity of an award presenter.

"I know you been having your doubts. You were black by default growing up around those white folks in the suburbs, but this move changed a few things. You finally got around us brothas and realized them rap tapes didn't make you black."

He pointed to my dresser, where hip-hop and alternative rock cassettes mingled freely in a plastic rack.

"Think about how far you've come," he said. "The basketball players in your history class stopped clowning you for asking why they call each other 'shorty.' You stopped wearing that Beastie Boys T-shirt you got at the beach." He shook his head sadly at my Raggedy Andy–looking 'fro. "If only we could get you to a barber on the regular."

I smiled sheepishly and touched my hair, my blackest feature.

"Still," Lucius continued. "You realized that dropping the 'g' from 'skateboarding' didn't make it any less white boy—" He held a palm up. "Now, I know, you been showing me these skateboard magazines. And they got some brothas in there. But it doesn't go down like that here in Richmond, V-A. We old-school Down South. 'Sides, you gotta know the rules before you break 'em."

I fought the urge to roll my eyes, and used my heel to nudge my skateboard further under the bed.

Lucius continued, hands joined inside his hoodie pocket, "I know you been going through some 'tragic mulatto' nonsense since you got here, feeling like no place is your place. But I see you working hard, and it's starting to come natural." Lucius paused, watching me whip fist to mouth a second too late to cover my grin, then said, "That's why I'm finally presenting you with *this*."

Triumphant horns blared as Lucius slowly drew his right hand from his pocket, thumped it on his heart, then held a wallet-sized laminated card up next to his face. A heart-swelling soul song kicked in and I craned forward.

BLACK CARD was written on the front in gold, diamond-encrusted capital letters. I reached for it, grinning, so happy to be a real brother. But Lucius pulled it close to his chest. "Hold up."

He turned my Black Card over in his hand as the music faded out.

"Brotha," he said, and sized me up.

I puffed my chest and ran my tongue across the front of my teeth.

"I hereby bestow you with this Black Card. Carry it with you, as proof that you're one of us, because . . ." He squinted and started to read from the back of the card, *"This card entitles the brotha or sista who bears it to all black privileges, including but not limited to: Use of the n-word, permission to wear flip-flops and socks, extra large bottles of lotion, use of this card as a stand-in for the Big Joker in a spades game, and, most important, a healthy and vocal skepticism of white folks aka crackers aka honkies. To be renewed in five years, upon evaluation."*

He nodded reverently, then pressed the card into my outstretched palm. His voice shook when he said, "Do well, brotha. Do well. Smoke the biggest blunts, kick the illest rhymes, and even when you're out rollin' around on that skateboard, remember that this," he folded my fingers over the card before taking his hand away, "is yours."

"Thank you," I said. "Thank you," and held the card for a moment before standing and slipping it into my pocket. It warmed my thigh.

The light went back to normal, but my room had a new type of sparkle. The unmade bed by the window was now part of a lineage of black people's unmade beds, the ball of colorful skateboard T-shirts on the floor by the closet were just like any black person might have. I smiled, satisfied. The world was starting to make sense.

Lucius put his arm around my shoulders and said, "Y'all havin' mac 'n' cheese for dinner?"

I pushed his hand off. "Nigger, we already ate. Always tryna—"

I could feel him freeze, so I turned. He squeezed the front of my hoodie into his fist. "It's nigg-a, not nigg-er. We don't say it like that."

Instantly, I was thrown back to every time I was scared I'd said the wrong thing around some black people, the thing that proved I didn't belong, that I liked rock music and didn't go to church, that I'd missed something important by living around white people. My hand slapped my front pocket. Lucius let go of my sweatshirt and pointed at my hand. "Maybe I was too quick in giving you that card. Maybe you got more to learn. Maybe," he narrowed his eyes, "you ain't a real brotha."

I stepped back, shaking my head, until paper crumpled under my butt and I was sitting on my desk.

"We'll see," he said. "You got it now, but you gotta maintain it."

BLACK CARD

SUMMER 2002

ONE

I was playing bass in a punk band called Paper Fire. We were popular enough in our sliver of the music scene that we could play to a basement full of people in most cities. On this night, we had a gig in Wilmington. We were rumbling down the interstate near the North Carolina border when the singer/guitarist Mason shouted, "Watcha doing up there?" from the driver's seat.

"He's doin' *black stuff*," Russell the drummer answered from shotgun.

I was lying in the plywood loft that stretches over our amps, drums, and guitars. I fired back a response that would have got me lynched fifty years earlier: "I'm lookin' out the back window for white women."

We all laughed.

We got "black stuff" from a comedy video we watched at a crash pad after a show in Pittsburgh. The comedian spotted a white man with a black woman in the crowd. In the nasal white guy voice that black comics do, he said, "This week, honey, we're doin' black stuff. We're going to see that new movie with the rappers in it and we're going to the Def Comedy Jam."

I'd recently started soaking up black pop culture, hoping for pointers, and this joke was the first time I could confidently call bullshit on what I heard. My black father's and white mother's interests overlapped naturally. They didn't have to plan individual racial fixes.

Still, when my white bandmates snickered across the couch at me, I knew I was stuck. "Doin' black stuff" became the answer to what I was up to when I was lost in thought. I wondered if the joke reminded them I was black, or helped them deal with the fact that there was something different about me and them, but I still liked it because it confirmed my blackness.

"Well, tell us if you see any good white women," Mason said, tapping the top of the steering wheel. "So we can protect 'em from you."

"What would Mona say to you checking out babes?" asked Russell.

"Nothing," I answered. "She's not my girlfriend."

Sigh.

"Who's Mona?" asked Mason, flicking his eyebrows in the rearview even though he'd had a girlfriend for over a year.

"We work with Mona," I said, hoping the subject would change. Dating a coworker usually ends with an unemployed person.

"Mona's tight," Russell said, and dragged on his cigarette.

I nodded, even though the guys weren't looking my way.

"Like, other girls are tight too," Russell said, then lowered the radio a bit. "But, you know how everyone always knows who cute girls are?" he asked.

"Sure, sure," said Mason. Richmond's a gossipy, small city. Dating is tricky.

"She didn't useta hang out with someone we know. She's no one's ex. She isn't even some classic girl that we'd always see working somewhere and wonder how we'd ever get to talk to her."

"She hot?" asked Mason.

"Yes," Russell and I said at once.

There was a pause while Mason waited for us to elaborate on our answers, and I thought about how there seemed to be a thin layer of cool water under Mona's skin, just enough to make me want to touch it and feel still.

Then I blurted out, "But she not, like, a hot girl. She's a cool girl. And that's more important."

Russell nodded and took another drag.

Mason shrugged.

Mona came up to my shoulder, and I could see where her shiny round dreadlocks escaped into her bandana. She drove a dusty Saturn, wore faded jeans, and kept skittery folk CDs in rotation at our coffee-shop job. In other words, Mona was a black hippie. I wish I knew more black hippies, because they set me at ease. They're basically a combination of my folks.

She started after this other hippie, who went by Nesta even though his paychecks said Ethan, quit to work at the new Ben & Jerry's ice cream place, which he called "B&G's." She was friendly to the awkward dudes who came in with their laptops, and the tips were higher, so I didn't mind that I'd always wind up mopping when we worked together.

Our first shift together, Mona stood about two inches closer than expected when I was showing her how to work the espresso machine. I caught myself staring at her reflection in the chrome, thinking we looked good next to each other, even when we were funny mirror distorted.

I hoped she'd like me if she knew I was black. My Prince CD came on the stereo and I said, "My dad loves this song." Then I listened to two seconds of utopian keyboard funk before saying, "My dad's black." Feeling less suave by the instant, I put my hand to the curls on top of my head and said, "People can't always tell."

She smiled, kept smoothing the plastic wrap on a plate of peanut butter cookies, and said, "I could tell."

She was covering my shift. I wondered if any of the regulars would be pleasantly surprised to see her instead of me. I texted her, *How are tips?*

Nap ruined, I wiggled out of the loft and sat on the bench seat behind Russell and Mason, rolling my stiff shoulders, watching Russell ash his smoke into a green plastic soda bottle. He's an easygoing, scruffy redhead who looks like he was born in a base-ball cap. We've drunk countless beers on the porch of the punk house where, at twenty-four, he's the oldest of six roommates.

Mason's a nervy, dark-haired guy with broad shoulders and sunken eyes. He always seemed to have an ulterior motive. We were technically roommates, but his girlfriend lived half a mile from us and had air-conditioning. You can guess where he tended to stay.

"One of you guys gonna ask her out?" Mason asked.

I opened my mouth but no sound came out. Russell got

busy shaking another cigarette from the pack in the cup holder. Mason chuckled and shook his head.

"Don't get jealous of each other," he said. "Don't break up the band."

"We won't," I said.

"I never went out with a black girl before," Russell blurted out.

"She's black?" Mason asked.

"Yeah." Russell nodded and took a drag.

I sat dreading the question I knew was coming next.

"How about you?" Mason asked me.

"Yes, I'm black."

"Nice try, dude," Mason said. "You ever dated a *sista*?"

"Man, you ever know him to date *anybody*?" Russell punched Mason's shoulder and the van wavered in the lane.

If I cussed him out, I'd have to prove him wrong, and I couldn't. It had been thirteen months, three weeks, and two days since I'd had sex. When I hit the one-year mark I told myself I was gonna give up on trying. Tell that to my body, though. That last girlfriend had been white, and she'd ended it because she was "looking toward life after college." The girl before her was white too, but dark and Jewish, which made me feel a bit better. And before her were a couple high school relationships that lasted a month each.

Except for a mixed girl I made out with in twelfth grade, none of these girls had been black. I did plenty of looking, got shot down a couple times, and never quite clicked with any black girls in high school—not their fault, I knew I was the odd man out. I'd been relieved to have the friends I had, even if most of them were white, but lately I'd been sure I was missing something.

I glared while Mason hooted at Russell's joke.

Then Mason said, "Like you should talk, Russell."

I laughed. Russell jabbed his cigarette into the air between us and said, "It doesn't work like that! He's clowning both of us!"

"He's just jealous because he's watching us players from the bench," I said.

Russell nodded.

"You players don't seem to be scoring," Mason said, and I leaned back in my seat, defeated. I'd heard that men date their mother's color. My dad disproved that theory, but it still made me feel a bit better when I got down on myself for not dating black women.

Russell looked out the window and smoked. Mason took a hand off the steering wheel and cranked the radio back up. A dancey rap song with chintzy synths roared over the engine.

"Yay-uhh," howled Russell, imitating one of the rappers.

I growled, "Get low, get low," like the other guy on the song. The synths kicked in and Mason murmured, "Get low . . . butts . . ." reverently, like his mind was in a strip club.

We were all quiet for a few seconds, then Russell lolled his head over at me and asked, "You ever had butt sex . . . with a girl?"

Mason gave the windshield a creepy smile and cut out around an eighteen-wheeler.

"No. No, I haven't." I sent a nervous grin to the windshield then asked, "You?"

He set the soda bottle ashtray in the cup holder and shuddered, almost offended I'd ask something so dumb. "No—"

"I mean, I'd try it," I said. "But the chance hasn't come up. And I'm not pushing for it."

"Ha," Mason said, and humped his seat like a dog scratching its ass on the rug. "'Pushing for it.'"

Russell leaned in, voice hushed like white people do when race comes up, "But I thought black guys fucked girls in the ass."

Suddenly, the radio cranked up louder. We all startled as the bass made the speaker covers buzz, and the van shook as we cut it close in front of the truck. Mason reached for the volume knob and it snapped off in his hand. He tossed it on top of the dashboard and clutched the steering wheel with both hands. A gleaming black luxury sedan shot up the highway and matched our speed in the right lane.

Our van's side door slid open as another *Yay-uhhh* blasted from the speakers. Wind roared in and the gray highway flew by between us and the fancy car. I gripped the back of Russell's seat, shouting, "Damn! What?"

The other car's back window slid open and Lucius rocketed out, drilling through the air between the vehicles. He landed next to me on the bench seat, slammed the van door, clapped his hands to his knees, and bellowed at Russell, "What did you just say, cracker?"

Russell threw his chin back in offense and whined, "Sorry."

I tried to smooth things over by saying, "Not that I'm aware of."

I hated to admit that, because then Russell could say, "Well, maybe if you were all black instead of half black, you'd do it." He stayed quiet, though, and Lucius turned to me and shouted, "Well?"

I wondered if Russell had some info that I didn't, so I asked, "Why do you think that?"

"Yeah," added Lucius. "That's foul."

Mason was sitting there, listening and driving.

"Well, just," Russell opened his hands to the road in front of him, "all the rap songs talk about booty and get low and you always hear about girls' butts, so I figured that's what it was all about." He had his hands spread in front of him, jiggling the biggest invisible booty in the world.

"No, man. No," I said. "The vagina is right there, too. You can reach it from behind. White guys' dicks go that far, right?"

Mason guffawed. Russell gave an embarrassed grin and nodded. Lucius fell sideways laughing, then hopped back to dap me up. The lines on the highway ahead glowed chalk-white in the overcast afternoon. I worried at how Russell was one of my closest friends and could still ask questions that made me feel so alone.

TWO Our show was at a dive in a part of Wilmington far from the chain restaurants and traffic that clogged southern cities in the '90s. The peak-roofed club looked like an old barn and smelled like one, if the animals smoked.

You'd think that the best shows would be in the biggest cities, but if you're in a lesser-known band like ours, you do better in smaller towns, where people aren't so jaded. They come out of the woodwork just because something's going on. That doesn't happen in places like New York and Los Angeles. People there have more options.

On the short stage, I peeked up from fiddling with my amp and saw a good fifty people already waiting. More were drifting in from the bar and parking lot, called by the twang and drone of our tuning. They seemed like our crowd: the weird kids, from "my first show" fifteen-year-olds in new cutoff army pants, to older guys in the sweet spot between high school and pain pills. Searchers, intent on finding their own fun. We were that fun, dug up online or passed along on a mix CD.

I ran through the slinky riff from Nirvana's "Come as You Are" to tune the A string to the E and looked to my bandmates for levels. My breath got short as my racial hang-ups and stage fright melded into a sun-hot beam that turned my fingers electric as we passed eye contact in a triangle and nodded, ready to blow off the long drive, the stupid week.

Mason was irritated about the shift-leader job he might as well quit.

Russell was ready to hit the drums so hard he'd get out of his dead-end life.

I wanted to turn a shade blacker every time I hit a bass string, envisioning a funk bassist with star sunglasses and a five-pointed bass; a jazz musician with his head back, the neck of his standup bass by his ear; even a lanky baseball pitcher folding himself into a crane shape on the mound before unleashing a fastball. Anything that read as black and performing.

I'd been playing shows for years. I was twenty-one and among the oldest people in the room. Still, I was hooked on the moment when the amps' hum faded, Russell sat back on his drum stool, and silence washed back through the crowd, loud and full, like a two-string power chord could burst it.

I held my breath as Mason said, "Hi, we're Paper Fire from Richmond, Virginia."

At that moment, everyone was on the same side. We all wanted four clicks of the drumsticks and twenty minutes of release. I wanted to disappear and sense how far my headstock pointed out so I didn't knock over a cymbal. I wanted to whip sweat from my forehead before it slicked up my bass, make eye contact with the knot of people up front headbanging and shaking their fists, and be amazed when they knew the lyrics Mason had written on a gas station napkin.

All the funk records I played at home, and I learned none of their rhythm by osmosis. In that punk band, my soul flailed and thrashed, and the room felt it more than heard it: a thick rumble that ripples out from the heart, shaking loose all the problems inside me.

THREE

My lips are full, my nose is broad, and my hair's a cloud of cinnamon. Usually, black people can tell that I'm black, because we know how to find each other in an unfriendly world. But white people see my green eyes and freckles and assume I'm white. They live in a world where they are the norm. Why would they expect me to be anything but?

Still, there's something about the way I look that gets black and white people to try to place me. This leads to what I call the "You Look Like" Game, where they explain my existence to themselves by telling me I look like someone else. The more they decide, the less control I have over my own personality.

Here are the "You Look Like" Game's top scorers:

Kid from Kid 'n Play

The light-skinned guy from a fun early '90s rap duo that did synchronized dances and starred in some movies that still pop up on cable. He was famous for his high-top fade, a cylinder of hair rising nine inches off the top of his head. He's also a mixed brother, and basically my color.

The good part about being told I look like Kid is that people love Kid 'n Play. No one's ever said, "You look like Kid 'n Play. I wanna fight those fools."

On the downside, I think white people are into old-school black stuff like Kid 'n Play because it's from the past, and can't change anything right now.

Embarrassing fun fact: I can't grab my ankle and jump over my leg to do Kid 'n Play's trademark dance.

Justin Timberlake

He's straight-up white, but has curly ramen hair, which I guess is where we sorta link up. He's also a great dancer with hit songs for days. I actually get called "Timberlake" a lot by black people, but mainly associate it with drunk white girls pushing up on me at dance parties. That's not necessarily a bad thing, and I'm jealous of how much black people like J.T.

Lenny Kravitz

He's handsome, half Jewish and half black, and dresses like he's from the '70s—he probably has a whole shelf just for the leather vests he wears with no shirt. We look nothing alike. This one bugs me. Out loud, I say it's because his music is bland and unoriginal. Truth is, I'm mad because he's beating me at my own game: he's got a better music career, money for cool vintage clothes, he looks blacker than me, and a couple of his songs are pretty ill.

"This light-skinned cat useta work with my sister at the supermarket"

This one's followed by an expectant look, like I should know the name of this random high-yella cashier. But not all mixed people know each other. We don't have brown bag parties where we listen to smooth r'n'b and make jokes about people working all day in the field. Sometimes I wish we did, though. Then I'd have someone to talk to about this stuff without feeling like a stereotypical halfie having an identity crisis.

Getting called "light-skinned" is a blessing and a curse, though. It's cool because it means I'm black, just paler than the average black person. Since being mistaken for white erases half of me, and happens so often that I think I've failed at blackness, I cherish being called black. Still, it also makes me feel like I have to reject my white side. That's why I feel guilty for loving punk rock.

FOUR

After our set, I spread Paper Fire's albums and T-shirts out on a sticky black table by the bar. Lucius presided over our merch from the back of the booth, the red-and-white beer light glowing off his white football jersey. He sipped a brown-bottled beer, actively ignoring me while I stood by the table. It was a good show, but he was clearly unhappy with the evening's demographics. A hundred people had watched us play, gawking, nodding their heads or bouncing on their toes, and they were all white, an ocean of moons spreading back through the small club.

A dozen boys crowded around the booth, bought a record or a shirt, clapped my sweaty shoulder, and said, "Nice show."

"Nice show" is a greeting and a compliment among the punks. You can only respond with a thanks or a self-deprecating, "But we (broke a string/messed up a bunch/played better last night)," because acting like you know you rock is to imply that you're above the audience, and that's not punk.

But it also means nothing. You could improvise an hour of free jazz country covers and everyone would still say, "Nice show."

I felt guilty for thinking something that snotty, and for

looking down on these kids for having a good time, and even for deciding that something that saved my ass as a teenager wasn't good enough now that I was old enough to buy beer.

By the time the record-buying crowd dispersed, Mason and Russell had moved all of our equipment offstage to the corner by the back door. After the last band, we'd form an assembly line and load the van, lingering by its open doors and chatting with the locals to see if there was a party.

I picked up the beer I'd been nervously sipping and sat by Lucius.

"Been a minute," I murmured, under the heavy metal that was pumping on the house system.

"Whose fault is that?" he asked.

I sipped again, still nervous.

"I see you takin' some steps," he continued. "But the records you play at home don't count for much. If you go out and you're the blackest one there," he gestured around the room, "it ain't black."

I sighed and nodded in agreement.

"And, it's the new millennium." He clapped on the last two words. "Why're you playing records, anyway? Ain't you got CDs?"

"I like records!" I said, waving my hand over the Paper Fire records. "They're cheap. And cool."

A punk kid walking past gave me a sarcastic thumbs-up.

Lucius rolled his eyes. "Look, being black is bigger than whether or not you play old-school soul at home or scream music for a bunch of teenagers at the club. You know your Black Card's set to expire. You ain't done much to keep it."

Heavy metal growled. I sighed.

"So, what do I do?" I asked, holding my head in my hand.

"Head to M.L.K. Boulevard and ask the first brotha I see if I can kick it?"

"No, man. No." He drummed his fingers on the table. "You gotta know you're black. Then the rest will fall into place. Every time I see you in a group of white folks, it looks like you're running from being black." He scissored his elbows like he was running. "It's time to stop, or it's gonna let you get away."

Since Lucius gave me the Black Card, I'd figured it was settled: I was black. I shook my head, starting to get worked up.

Mona would quiet this static in my head. This was my first time out of town since I'd started crushing on her, and I kept scanning the room for that soft baby-blue T-shirt she wears, willing her to appear with that Tupperware of salad she'd always bring to our shifts. Instead, I saw a room full of punks, mainly male, all white. I slugged my beer and wiped the condensation from my hand on the thigh of my damp jeans.

I pulled my phone out of the little shoulder bag I'd carried into the show.

> *Mona 7:43 pm*
> *Tips were ok. How was your concert?*

It's called a show and I loved that she didn't know that.

> *9:45 pm*
> *Pretty good. Think we're going to a party next.*
> *Thanks for covering my shift.*

JJ, the bassist for Kill All Their Infernal Soldiers, the local band whose name was longer than their songs, walked up. He skipped the southern summer punk uniform of limbless black tees and work pants in favor of a dirtbag raver look, featuring a scraggly goatee, faded baggy jeans, and a visor from a fast-food pizza place. We'd snuck a couple beers in his hatchback during the nine-piece high school ska band who'd opened the show, and he'd told me about his funk side project. The fact that he stood out, even in a goofy way, made me like him and even wonder if his funk friends weren't white. Sometimes I get jealous of white dudes with black friends because, hey, if they can pull it off, why can't I?

"Nice show, by the way," he said.

"Thanks."

"So, I think y'all are staying at my place tonight," he said.

"Cool, thank you."

I immediately started guessing what his spot was like. It's a reflex after going on a couple of tours. You look at your host's grooming and guess how dirty their floor will be. If they're smoking, you assume they do it inside and that your sleeping bag will stink the next day. If they say they're having a party, you hope they live in a big house so you can get loaded fast then sneak upstairs to sleep. He wasn't smoking and he had a quiet air of having his act together, but I couldn't get a read on him.

"Well, not *my* place." He shrugged. "I live with my dad."

"Oh, cool."

Parents' houses meant clean and quiet, extra beds and blankets, and an adult who might cook cheese eggs in the morning.

"Well, not really *cool*," he said.

**FIVE** Sober Mason drove, gunning it to stay with JJ, who took wide turns on the suburban corners. I sat shotgun, palming the dash for balance. Behind me, Russell shouted over the engine in a slow, hippie drawl, "Heyyy, mannn, think JJ likes weeed?"

I turned and said, "I hope so, brahhh."

We both drooped our eyelids and nodded slow and groovy, pinching invisible hookah hoses.

Lucius went, "Pssh."

Mason said, "Just be coool when we get theeere, bros. This is JJ's daaad's house and he might be a naaarc, maaan."

He was using the same voice as us, but somehow he sounded like the narc.

Last fall, Mason saw this hippie freshman guy perched on the steps of the college library, smoking a four-hose hookah by himself. Mason cracked up Russell and me with an impression of him, and it wasn't until later that I thought about how hookahs have a few hoses, and there's something very lonely about smoking one alone. Still, whenever weed comes up, my bandmates and I pretend to be the Hookah Guy.

———

We coasted to a stop in front of a brown ranch house. JJ's band-mate Tim, an uptight guy with a pointy chin and suspiciously new guitar, pulled up next. We were the only signs of life on the sleepy street, so we left our stuff in the van and single-filed into the backyard through a gate in the tall wood fence. Waiting under a safety light by the back door, I watched Lucius emerge into the yard last, shoulders hunkered forward, looking around and nodding slow.

Mona wasn't there, and I was jealous of all of Richmond for having the chance to see her that night.

A teenager who shared JJ's horse jaw and curve of goatee sat spread-kneed in a lawn chair, pursing his lips to spit into a plastic fast food cup. A middle-aged man in an open Hawaiian shirt sprawled in the next chair, an arm's length from an aboveground pool. The dad was the swarthy, 1970s version of handsome, with broad shoulders and a mustache. Lucius and I both thought of the rerun detective shows we'd watched while skipping school, guys like this, smart-talking ladies' men who could take a punch. What would it be like to have a dad who checked out your girlfriends?

"What's up, Dad? I brought some guests. They're gonna crash here tonight," said JJ.

"OK, then," said Dad.

When he stood to shake hands, he tottered over the beer cans at his feet like a movie monster over a model city. He turned to JJ's little brother and said, "You ain't gonna say hello?"

The kid nodded, "'Sup," the shadow under his ball cap shortening to reveal a constellation of zits.

"Aw, he's mad because he's grounded tonight and has to hang out with his pop," said the father.

The kid's brim went down and his face disappeared.

JJ made a couple trips to a pool house shed, passing out folded lawn chairs, then opening a mini-fridge and underhanding us beers. He opened the last one with the pointer finger of the hand that was holding it, then curled it up to drink as he hopped onto a red picnic table on the far side of the pool. A volley of pops filled the night as we opened our beers, too.

I checked for a text from Mona and the dad gave my phone a long look. I put it back in my pocket and he swept his eyes over us, "Y'all gonna catch some surf tomorrow?"

"We weren't planning on it. Might hit the beach, though," Mason said.

Dad nodded approval and burped into the top of his fist.

"You surf a lot, JJ?" I asked, and my voice echoed off the water in the pool between us. I'd never surfed before, and I live up to one black stereotype: I'm a horrible swimmer.

"When the waves aren't too shitty," he answered.

The kid piped up, "Imma go tomorrow. JJ, can I borrow your board? Mine's cracked."

"If you don't get that thing fixed, you're gonna sink like a nigger in the water," rumbled Dad.

Father and sons had roostery southern drawls, mixed with a surfer's long vowels. "Nigger" came out in three syllables, "Nee-yuh-gir," and it traveled across the pool loud enough to knock me back in my chair.

After a whole life in the south, I was still shocked when I heard white people use that word. And this guy had said it loud enough for the neighbors to hear. Did the neighbors say "nigger" too? Casually, in small talk?

I could see them meeting on the driveway while picking up the morning newspaper.

"Good morning, Tom. Let's see what's happening in the world today," the father would say.

"Mornin'. I wonder if there's any nigger news in the Metro section," the neighbor would answer, unsheathing the paper from its plastic sleeve.

"Must be. Niggers are always up to something," the father would say, padding his way back into the house in black bedroom slippers with stuffed, red-mouthed Sambo heads over the toes.

The kid didn't miss a beat and shouted, "Shit, Dad. I swim better'n a nigger, and you know it!"

Lucius was to my right, sitting stock still like a cat about to pounce. I hid my eyes by looking at the rippling pool water, feeling my bandmates' attention turning toward me like it was my job to say something; seeing Tim and JJ fidgeting, probably worried that the cool out-of-town guys would tell everyone that their band was racist; JJ's eyes shifting until he finally says, "Y'all. Come on."

The dad looked up. "What? We boring you?"

"We've got guests."

"Oh, we *embarrassing* you?" said the dad, belly straining his half open shirt when he leaned back to drain his drink.

JJ just sighed and looked down. I wondered how many years

it took for him to realize it was wrong for his dad to say "nigger." Or even how his pop explained to him that they could talk like that at home, but not at the supermarket. I doubted his dad was trying out the n-word for the first time this night.

I felt sorry for JJ. I also didn't trust him anymore and set my beer down at the same time that JJ's dad told the little brother, "And don't think I didn't hear you cussing. Watch your mouth, 'less you want another night at home."

I was pissed off and scared at being stuck behind a tall fence with a couple of bigots, wondering what would change if I popped out of my chair and yelled, "I'm black, dammit. Where do you get off talking like that?"

If they said, "Sorry, we didn't know," it would make things worse. Then my suspicions would be confirmed; that so many white folks had a moment at parties when they scanned the room before getting all racial.

It would also mean that they couldn't tell that I was black, which knocks the breath out of me whenever it happens.

If they could tell, it would be horrifying. Because then they'd be tempting Lucius and me with retaliation, waiting for us to jump up and start shouting or hit someone so they could fight back or call the cops.

If they said, "We've just realized the error of our ways," I wouldn't believe them.

And who was I to them, anyway? Just some guy in their yard tonight, down the interstate and probably getting pulled over tomorrow.

If they said, "Well then, get off my property, nigger," I'd have to decide how much faith I had in my bandmates. Would they follow me to the van? But what would be solved then? We'd drive to an all-night diner, furious, and this family would kick back, enjoying the extra space in their backyard, and go back to filling the night with "niggers."

Lucius alone would stand up and say something ultracool like, "Hope y'all little men are happy back here with your pool. I've got big things to do," before disappearing into the dark. And I felt that same impulse, Lucius trying to take the wheel in my body, getting heated when I held on and sat there, having these thoughts, taking a deep breath and realizing I couldn't sleep in that house.

Just like that, the moment passed and it was too late to yell. I hated myself all the more for being so gutless. Maybe when I got home, the used classic rap CDs I'd bought a couple years after the fact would be gone, and my father would be blond.

Lucius sat in the shadow of the safety light, his white-and-orange basketball shoe tapping in the grass. Father and sons kept on, but all I could hear coming from their mouths was the word "nigger."

"Nigger nigger nigger?" JJ asked his brother.

"Ha, nigger," answered the young guy.

"Now, nigger nigger," the father chimed in.

I could see each utterance of "nigger," in graffiti-style red bubble letters, in an austere black font, in a yellow comic book explosion. The "niggers" swirled around and stayed, blocking my sight, until all three guys' voices joined, chanting, "Nigger . . . nigger . . . nigger," growing louder than the blood rushing in my ears.

Tim stood up. "I know a bar."

SIX

The gravel lot was full of pickups, mostly new and clean. Lucius hooked my elbow and pulled me aside as the others entered the bar, twangy music disappearing with the door's thump.

"What was that?" he asked, face all hat brim and shadow.

"I don't know, man. Those guys were—"

"Naw." He poked my chest. "You. What were *you* doing there?"

"I was . . . I didn't know what to do."

"Yeah, I could tell." He looked down and away and wheeled back. I flinched, scared he was gonna swing at me. He shook his head, weaving on the little sidewalk by the door.

"What *should* I have done?" I asked.

Lucius stilled and looked at me again, hand out. "Give it to me."

"What?"

"I said, give it to me," he hissed.

"Give you what?"

The frustration from earlier was bubbling up, making me shout.

A top-heavy white guy with nicotine yellow hair and a

tucked-in plaid shirt stepped out into the night and looked our way. I gave him a nod like you do when you get caught arguing with your girlfriend. He tucked his chin, dragged on his cigarette, and swiveled into the lot, gravel crunching as he made tracks to his truck.

"This ain't your first time playing dumb tonight," said Lucius. His hand was still out, brown skin smudgy in the neon beer light.

"Not that."

"Yes," he said.

My hand flew to my hip pocket, covering my wallet, where my Black Card rested between a sub-shop punch card and my old student ID.

"No." I stepped back. Lucius followed. "It hasn't expired yet."

"Don't matter," he said. "It's not yours no more. You let those crackers act a fool and didn't say a damn thing. Your pale, mixed ass just sat there like some sorta white boy. So, that's what you are. You ain't black no more."

I thought of every hip-hop listening session, the talks my pop gave me about police, how choked up I got reading *Autobiography of an Ex-Colored Man*.

Now I was an ex-colored man. Dad was a couple hundred miles away, growing paler in the moonlight, his scissor-cut 'fro straightening. Had I ever been a colored man?

I sighed and slid the card out of my wallet, eye lingering on the last black privilege:

. . . *most important, a healthy and vocal skepticism of white folks aka crackers aka honkies.*

That was the clincher. I handed him the card, eyes welling up.

It wasn't fair. I might have just had my chance to prove my blackness, but every other chance I'd blown had led up to that moment. Every little bit of black life I missed while out in the suburbs, until I got so nervous that I'd be rejected for not being black enough, that I clenched up and turned it into a self-fulfilling prophecy. And from every run-in with the cops to this mess of a night, I'd had plenty of time to grow skeptical of white folks' acceptance. Instead, I'd dug in deeper, until I wound up handing over my Black Card outside a North Carolina country bar.

I was useless to black people. White people only wanted me when they thought I was white, or when they needed some entertainment. I'd show everyone. I shoulder-checked Lucius as I stepped into the bar with a powerful thirst.

The music didn't scratch to a stop or anything, but I caught eyes sliding across me and tensed, wondering if this was a night where all strange white folks were as racist as JJ's family.

That "Earl had to die" country song was playing, but it sounded different from the radio. At the back of the room were two long-faced white women with perms, one in a wheelchair, the other bent to share the microphone, singing in lazy unison. It was karaoke night. I smiled. How was I gonna reclaim what I'd lost? How could I make karaoke night at an all-white country bar a black experience?

The place was homey and not quite a dive, wood-paneled and crowded with people in their thirties and older. Lucius passed me, headed to an empty barstool by the bathrooms.

I joined my bandmates at the middle of the bar. Mason had the bartender pouring a row of whiskeys while Tim from the local band leaned on a stool and talked to a woman with pulled-high jeans.

Russell raised an eyebrow. "So . . ."

I nodded and said, "So . . ." too.

"Those people were real," Russell paused, "hicks."

"You mean racist?" I asked.

It came out sharper than I expected and, for once, I didn't smooth out the anger with a laugh. I took a moment to relish the pause that gave Russell. Angry black man in the house! Angry ex-black man in the house!

I shook my head like Lucius had done outside and asked Russell, "What should I have done, man?"

"I dunno. What can you do? Tell them they're racist? What'll that do?" He scanned the room and quietly said, "Hicks are hicks."

I didn't like hearing more justifications coming from someone else's mouth. I didn't like that I didn't think to ask Russell what he should have done.

Mason handed me a drink and said, "We might as well enjoy *something* tonight."

I clammed up. Mason only cares about getting famous, and that makes me not trust him. As I took my first sip of what had probably been our gas money, the song ended and the KJ took the mic. He was overweight, with a baseball cap puffed up on his head and aviator-style glasses.

"That was 'Goodbye, Earl,'" he said, and his tone reminded me of when guys argue about sports. "Next up, we have a little CCR."

A guy with thinning hair and a black mustache skidded up, grinning, and took the mic. A synth version of the guitar lick from "Fortunate Son" booped and beeped through the speakers and he twisted his wrist like he was revving a muscle car's ignition. A table of folks near the door hooted. It was clear that he sang this song every dang week.

Some more booze. I could feel Lucius across the room, sliding his thumb across the edge of my Black Card, waiting for me to redeem myself. I palmed the binder of songs. I knew what I was gonna do.

**SEVEN** After fifteen minutes, most of which were occupied by a very sincere '70s rock power ballad from a very divorced-looking guy, the KJ stepped back up. "And next we have 'It's Tricky,' by Run-DMC."

Run-DMC's *Raising Hell* was my first record. One afternoon, I saw guys rapping about math on a kids' TV show. The next day in my third-grade class, I was talking about how awesome it was, when this white girl named Claire, who wore hoop earrings and was preternaturally cool for an eight-year-old, said, "Oh, you like rap? Do you like DMC?"

I put down my safety scissors that didn't cut, briefly wondered if DMC was the nation's capital, then said, "I don't know."

"They're rap." She smiled. "My babysitter plays their tape."

I was distraught at the idea of someone knowing about something cool before me. It was my first moment of geeky jealousy. I had to hear this rap group.

That night over dinner, I asked my father if he'd heard DMC. He chewed spaghetti. "Hmm, no."

And I learned that there was music out there that even Dad, of the infinite records, couldn't play me.

Later that week, I came home from school and the first thing I saw, propped up on the table in the hall, was this purple-and-green record with two black guys in leather jackets and gangster fedoras on the cover. The guy on the left wore big square glasses and deadpanned the camera, like he'd just made his point and dared you to disagree. The guy on the right had his eyes down, a swing in his stride, nodding, "Mmm hmm," to back up the guy in the glasses.

What were they talking about?

Dad swooped in from the kitchen and led me over to the stereo, balanced by the living room window on a stack of particleboard crates. "They're not just called DMC," he said. "They're called Run-DMC. I guess that's their names."

"Which one is DMC?" I asked.

Dad was already sliding the record out of the sleeve and into his rough brown hands. "I don't know. The clerk didn't tell me that."

He put the needle down and it was just two voices, louder than I was allowed to speak at home. The first guy shouted, "Now Peter Piper picked peppers," then the other guy chimed in, "But Run write rhymes."

They went back and forth a couple more times, then these big drums with bells kicked in. Dad moved to block the record player, a habit from years earlier when I'd dance to kids' music.

I was into it. I'd like to imagine that I started perfectly pop-locking, but I probably just flailed. Grade school me was mad skinny, and let's start at the top: red mulatto 'fro, untouched by the new hairbrush on my dresser; giant tortoiseshell glasses kinda like DMC's; a pocket T-shirt, probably turquoise; sweatpants with knee patches; and tie-dyed Chuck Taylors picked by my hippie mother. I was a wild-looking geek.

My mom and I had already bonded over funny books and sticky craft projects at the dining room table, but Run-DMC showed me how interested Dad was when I talked about music. They were the impetus for me asking for my own record player, and Dad pulling his old one from the attic. The beginning of seeking black art, wanting it to teach me lessons about myself.

After a week, I could recite the lyrics to my favorite song, "It's Tricky," a capella, but even after years of playing music in front of people, I was nauseated, scared to do it in this bar.

The following things could go down:

1. My high school could assemble for an early reunion and clown me for rapping white, inspiring Lucius to borrow scissors from the bartender and cut my Black Card into long, curly strips.

2. Some rap-hating white guy in overalls could lynch me out back, then Lucius would catch me swinging and slip my Black Card back into my pocket.

3. A scene from a trite comedy, where uptight old people dance to rap, and a grandma character declares something like, "When I get home, I'm going to have Fred put it in *his* mouth!"

4. I could channel my nerves into an enthusiastic performance where I assert my blackness by karaokeing a rap song, but get ignored by a bar full of middle-aged white folks.

5. I could just do it, and be black. Which I am. Sorta. Or was.

———

The spotlight made the short stage a boxing ring.

Holding the mic on the other side of his gut, the KJ stopped me with a hand on my arm and said, "Keep it clean, now."

I told him, "I'll stick to what's on the monitor."

He handed me the mic and disappeared into shadow, followed by the rest of the bar. When Paper Fire played earlier, the whole room took a deep breath as we counted off our first song. Here, there was chatter, and a woman laughing separate syllables, "Haw . . . Haw . . . Haw . . ." over the clink of glasses.

I eyed the torso-high blue screen floating a yard to my right. The first lyrics appeared in white, "This speech is my recital / I think it's very vital." There were four beats of shakers redone in dinky MIDI then I started rapping, as, letter by letter, beat by beat, the words turned yellow on the screen. I heard my voice echoing through the PA, deep and sorta nasal, always with a touch of smartassedness, a southern softness in the vowels, sounding white? Black? Maybe both or neither, like a newscaster.

I couldn't see the crowd, but they'd gone quiet. I stared into the glare, rapping the lyrics that I'd memorized years before, remembering the green rug of my old bedroom, the neighbor's cream-colored house as seen through the window above the spinning record. As the music faded, I churned butter with my arms, doing a quick Cabbage Patch dance, and the room burst into applause.

I was a black man dancing for the white folks. I was a white guy cheekily doing black dances from ten years ago. I was blacking up by singing a song off the record credited with bringing rap to the suburbs. Even my attempts at acting black were white.

Still, the applause made me proud of myself. But if I smiled too much, the bar would know that crushing a rap song at karaoke wasn't an everyday thing for me. Plus, I was nervous about what would come next. I made a beeline for the bar, where I'd last seen my bandmates. Tim was smiling admiration and still clapping. Mason had that "frontman watching his bassist get attention" smirk.

I said, "Maybe we should go?" and Russell shook his head and patted me on the back, handing me a fresh drink. My dry mouth wrung water from the whiskey.

A woman began singing a slow country song. I looked for Lucius and felt a touch on the back of my neck. When I turned, a drunk blonde in her early thirties slid her hand to my shoulder like a middle school slow dance and said, "That was just great, brother."

I started to thank her but she cut me off, "We're signing you up for more."

She looked to her left, where one of her friends, also drunk, was looking back and forth between the binder of songs and the sign-up sheet, pen scribbling.

I snuck a peek at Lucius. He was still in his seat, holding up a cognac glass so it glowed in the Christmas lights around the bar mirror. What was blacker? To do the bidding of these women and sing some rap songs, or to tell them to go to hell?

I broke for her friend. "Oh no, I just got done—"

The first woman grabbed my arm. "You know 'Baby Got Back,' right? That's our song, and you're gonna do it."

The friend finished signing me up, pushed the clipboard away, and said, "My friend thinks you look like that rapper from the movie."

I pictured a gangsta rapper in a '90s hood flick. She waved

her flattened hand a few inches above her center part. "The guy with the big hair. *Dance Party* or something. It's always on cable."

"Right," I said. "Good movie."

It was weird to be a black dude who'd just been told by the only other black dude at the bar that he wasn't black anymore, and to be getting signed up for the only rap song that all white people know, by this woman who kept calling me "brother." I assumed she could tell I was black, and I was proud. My blacking up was succeeding.

The whiskey warmed my ears and upped my confidence. I'd sung a song and not been beaten up. Most weekends, I wanted to make some drunk woman happy. Why not now?

I said, "Fine. But you gotta buy me a drink."

EIGHT

Round Two:

The KJ handed me the mic, mid eyeroll. The Valley Girl spoken intro, "Oh. My. God. Becky. Look at her butt," began. I stood there like a dick, then jumped a mile when hands snaked up from behind and clamped my chest. I wheeled around, arm cocked to thump someone with the microphone and what did I see? The drunk blonde, pulling her head back to avoid the mic, hands still on my chest, "It's OK, brother. I'm just gonna grind on you while you rap," like it was business as usual.

Have you ever been scared and horny at the same time? It takes you back to seventh grade real fast. I imagined the same overalls-wearing phantom hick slamming the tavern door open after railing some crank in the parking lot. As his tweaked-out eyes adjusted to the dim bar, he'd see his wife's empty chair. Then his ears would pick up some horrendous jungle music and, with disgust, he'd look for the ape that's singing it . . . only to find his wife up there doing that sexy dance they saw on MTV.

The bass line started vamping under the intro. There was rhythmic clapping from the bar, probably my bandmates. Time was running out. I told her, "I don't think your husband would like this," hoping that the answer would be, "I'm not married," followed by a flirty squeeze on the chest.

Instead, she said, "Oh, he's not here tonight."

At least I got the chest squeeze.

The song kicked in and so did I. Like anyone who listened to the radio in the early '90s, I knew the words to this PG-rated ode to big asses. Her crotch and butt bumped my ass and thighs, always off-beat, getting surprisingly close to the backs of my knees. During the breaks, I'd turn to see the blonde gyrating, but I didn't dance with her. Where was her husband? Were his friends here?

The song ended to applause and she disappeared. I turned to head back to the bar. Lucius flicked an "I'm watching you" eyebrow. My path was blocked by two middle-aged parrotheads who had slid their chairs back and sat smiling, showing teeth. On the round table between them was a phalanx of empty highball glasses.

The man, heavy, with a mullet and Hawaiian shirt, said, "That was cool, man."

The woman just smiled in her lacy black blouse. I shook the man's hand. His palms were soft, the chunk between thumb and forefinger, meaty.

"We wanna get you a drink," he said.

"Uh, OK."

We started chatting and I told them I was down from Richmond.

"Where are you sleeping tonight?" he asked.

Backyard full of crackers, the n-word floating in an

aboveground pool, Tim complaining about his girlfriend in a way that made it clear we couldn't stay with them . . .

"Ya know, I dunno," I said.

I was drunk enough to not care if I sounded black, and heard a voice hoarse from singing and liquor.

The wife was still smiling, eyes sinking from my face as she said, "Why don't you stay with us? We have a hot tub and more cocktails."

The man smiled slowly as his wife's eyes stopped at my crotch. The seventh-grade feeling washed over me again. I downed my drink, then was saved by the blonde, who informed me it was time to sing "The Humpty Dance."

I let her pull me by the wrist. Third time could be the charm and I could get my card back. Mason cut us off at the pass and said, "Hey, it's time to go. We're just gonna head back to Richmond."

Lucius was gone from his stool, his bell-shaped cognac glass empty next to a couple of heavy-bottomed beer glasses. I followed.

The blonde said, "Hey."

I said, "Bye," and saluted.

Outside, the song's sliding bass line rumbled through the walls. No one was rapping. I crawled over Lucius and back into the loft, stealing a glance at the country road between his corn-rows as the van rolled out onto smooth pavement.

"You're telling me 'Baby Got Back' *isn't* about buttfucking?" Russell teased from the front seat.

"Shut up," I grumbled into the carpet that Mason had stapled to the top of the loft, then pulled my phone out of my backpack and looked at it for the first time in hours.

Mona 9:46 pm
You're welcome. Don't trash any hotel rooms
hahaha

I couldn't think of a clever or honest answer to that, and fell asleep with my mind in the huge gap between what people think touring is like, and the reality.

I woke up two hours later, dry-mouthed and stale, feeling the van slowing as we exited the highway. Russell was rapping along with the radio, "Every day I pray I don't pull the trigger. Are you trying to die?" And Mason joined him to boom, "Uh-uh! No, nigga!" as he hit the brake one last time to stop.

I flashed mad. My head thunked the roof as I popped up and shouted, "Really?"

The engine died and my voice echoed through the van. They sat still in their seats.

"Haven't we heard that word enough?" I asked.

"I thought you liked rap," said Mason.

"Oh, I do," I said. "And I see that you do, too." White guys love rap because they can sing along and have an excuse to say the n-word. "But I don't like hearing that word out of white people's mouths," I said extra loud as Lucius stirred awake in the seat below me. "You don't get to say it."

In the past, I'd talked to them about being black, but had never drawn a line and said something serious about white people, because I was scared someone would say what Russell said right then, "But you're half white, dude."

I pushed on, fast. "You ever hear me saying 'nigger'?" I asked, hands curling over the edge of the loft. The word has never sounded right coming out of my mouth. This time it squeaked. No one answered, and my disappointment with Russell caught up.

Mason murmured, "But it was on the radio."

"I don't care," I said. "You sound too damn happy when you sing along."

And with that, I slithered down from the loft, hoping Lucius would hand me my Black Card as I exited through the side door. He didn't.

We'd stopped at this Tijuana-themed tourist trap called Mexico Way. It's painted as if some ignorant white folks tried to make a whole town out of old-timey Mexican stereotypes. I walked to the restroom, in a low building painted to look like adobe.

Mariachi horns whined through hidden speakers, echoing in the dim concrete bathroom. I was still wired up and angry, alone while Mason pumped gas and Russell hit the store for a soda and some smokes. I'd have to rejoin them soon. Why couldn't I just confront racism when it was convenient—at the end of a shift, or from someone who was about to drive off forever? I knew why. I'd had the chance earlier and blown it.

I washed my hands in cold water, then stepped back outside and saw that our van was parked under a giant concrete sombrero. Mexico Way's mascot is a cartoon named José who wears a sombrero and has word bubbles over his head, written in a phonetic Mexican accent, urging "joo" to buy everything from fireworks to nachos and acrylic blankets. There's a motel, but it must be impossible to sleep under so much neon.

BLACK CARD / 51

Mexico Way is what Mexico is to the south. And, to Wilmington, North Carolina, I was hip-hop. All this time I'd spent trying to learn to be black by listening to rap and soul records, and the only time it had gone over was in a room full of old white folks.

I crept back into the van and feigned sleep. A minute later, I heard a door slam and Mason asked, "Everyone in?"

Russell grunted, "Yeah," and the van's engine started.

My Black Card was still close, but not in my pocket.

SUPERHERO
ORIGIN STORY

 "Muhfukka."

"Motherfucker."

"Naw, *Muhh*-fukka."

"Mothafucka."

Lucius sighs. "Muhhh. Fuh-kka."

"Muthah fuckah?"

"The first part's just 'muhh.' Ain't no t-h. Muhh."

"Muhh?"

"Yeah. Now work it in."

"Muhh fuckah."

"Let it roll, though. Muhfukka."

"Muhfukka."

"Yeah, but feel that 'uhh' in your stomach. Not your nose. Don't say it so white."

TWO We lived in the DC suburbs and, at my white school, the fourth-grade-boy Mount Rushmore was Bart Simpson's serrated paper bag head and the five long-haired, cigarette-smoking skulls from the Guns N' Roses logo. My mom was cool enough to buy me T-shirts of both, and I'd wear them on special occasions, like when we drove the half hour to dinner at Dad's childhood friend Kenny's apartment.

I liked Kenny's living room because I could look out the balcony door and see a parkway, with tall trees waving in the glow of passing headlights. I imagined every car going somewhere interesting. That didn't happen at home, where I'd kneel backwards on the couch, peering out the window and counting the times one of the neighborhood dads jogged around the block, grinning and waving as he passed.

When we'd come off the elevator for our last visit, we'd found Kenny clutching a frosty beer glass in his building's carpeted hallway. He'd grinned and shouted, "No niggers allowed!" at my dad, who folded into a convulsive laugh I'd never seen him do.

The elevator door slid shut behind us. Mom's mouth was a circle and she rotated her wrists, trying to decide if she should cover my ears or her mouth or Kenny's. I knew that "nigger" was the worst bad word, but had never heard someone say it before that night. When Kenny's eyes slid to my mom, his grin turned embarrassed and he said, "I'm sorry, y'all come on in."

Kenny's daughter, Jada, and I had an easy friendship that we'd renew at the kids' table over our hatred of greens, but it felt different now that I was ten and the word "girl" had a capital G. Over the past year, I'd heard the n-word in a couple of rap songs and wondered if Kenny would make Dad laugh like that again, but the hall was empty when we arrived. In their apartment, Mom went into the kitchen, wine bottle first, and started laughing with Jada's mom, Pam. Dad and I followed Kenny to the living room, where he stood in front of the balcony door, his hand on the back of a chair, and gave me the standard "You got so big!" treatment that's so hard to respond to.

That year, my hands and feet felt huge and I didn't know where to put them, so I smiled sheepishly. Then Kenny squinted at my T-shirt, seeing the Guns N' Roses skulls at the tips of an ornate cross, with the redheaded singer at the crux, and asked, "What's this? The, uh, Grateful Dead?" as if remembering a phrase from another language.

"No, Guns N' Roses," I said, incredulous.

"Sorry, I don't know much rock 'n' roll," he said.

"It's awesome."

I knew that something that made rock music cool was that adults didn't always like it, but I sensed something else going on when Kenny shot a knowing glance at Dad.

Jada appeared in the doorway to the small hall, light from

her bedroom catching the ringlets of lace in her white dress. At dinner, she took careful bites and talked about grades and church, two things that weren't to my interest. She was trying to fit into something that I was trying to escape and I didn't understand why.

THREE

Save for a couple of suburbanites, the black kids at my grade school arrived early in a bus from the city, and left together on that same bus, a submarine that dunked into the ocean beyond the Beltway every morning. The busing program was called EDCO and, at school, EDCO meant black. When my white classmates saw my dad they'd ask if I was an EDCO kid, forgetting that, unlike the kids who were bused out, I played in the soccer league with them, went to their birthday parties, and walked home from school.

In fifth grade, we did a heritage unit and the first assignment was to find out what countries our ancestors came from. I asked my parents at the dinner table and my mom said, "Ireland," and my dad said, "Umm . . ."

"Africa?" Mom asked.

"That's a continent," I said.

"Probably Africa," Dad said.

I showed up the next day to find orange slips of paper hanging on the board by the classroom door. Each one had the name of a European country, with lines for kids' names underneath. On the far right, next to Russia, was one that said Africa. We went around the room and each kid read off their countries. Germany and Ireland filled up fast, trailed closely by Italy and France, and then two kids' names under Africa, Naima and Anthony, EDCO kids.

My white classmates said, "Huh?" and "Why is your name on Africa?" as our teacher added my name.

"Because my dad's from there."

I started sitting with Naima and Anthony. Naima was taller than me, with glasses and big twisted pigtails. During group projects, she'd tell me what I'd missed on *In Living Color*, the raunchy black comedy show that my mom wouldn't let me watch anymore, using its new later airtime as an excuse. Naima had a laid-back older-sister personality, while Anthony was a sly instigator with a slanting Bobby Brown Gumby haircut and a pinkie-length braided rattail.

Once a week, our class would join another and their homeroom teacher would darken the room and read a novel about the Revolutionary War to us in a monotone. I was dreading it the second time we went in, and was happy to see an empty seat near the door, by Naima and Anthony. When nothing but sunshine lit the room, and the teacher had started droning on about muskets, Anthony poked my rib and pointed to the classroom door, which he'd nudged open with the toe of his sneaker. I was just old enough to want to climb through holes in fences, and followed without worrying, crawling out of the classroom and finding Naima and Anthony pressed up against the wall in the hall outside the door.

We ran down four flights of stairs to this big, rarely used bathroom by the gym in the basement. Sneakiness was the main thrill. Being away from class with my friends. Having it not be a big deal that a girl was in the boys' room. Stifling our laughs and footsteps so they didn't echo off the high ceiling. We took turns standing on a toilet and climbing onto this ledge behind the stalls, to peek out a window to the street.

We snuck off to the bathroom a couple more times, then one day a boy was in one of the stalls when we climbed up to look out the window. He was our age but looked tiny sitting on that toilet while Anthony barked at him to get out and Naima told Anthony to chill. We didn't get caught, but our teacher must have known because a couple days later he got me alone in the hall and declared, "People will judge you by who you hang around with. People notice these things."

I had liked my teacher until that day, when I pretended not to get what he was saying, but my mind went to the thing that had animated my year, my friendships with Anthony, who had given me an old AC/DC tape saying, "I got this and thought it was something else. You like this stuff, right?" and Naima, who'd said, "No, he's mixed, he looks like you," when I'd said that one of the guys from the rap group Kid 'n Play was white.

In a bid to get my mom to let me watch *In Living Color* again, I'd relay stories about the show from Naima. This backfired. My mom started teasing me for having a crush, drawing out the vowels of Naima's name, "Did you talk to Naiiieeemahh today?"

At school, it was only OK to like one of a select few richer white girls with long hair, scuffed canvas sneakers, black satin jackets from the tryout soccer league, and the occasional makeup. Naima wasn't one of those girls, who made me nervous and sarcastic. She felt like home and I liked her, but to realize that would be to admit that I wasn't one of the popular kids, and to further understand that I was a black kid.

Anthony went somewhere else for middle school and Naima and I drifted apart over the long summer. In sixth grade, she started dating an eighth grader and would wave sometimes when we passed in the hall, where I usually walked alone.

FOUR

I spent most of middle school skateboarding, then in high school, my dad lost his job and the three of us moved to Richmond. The guy who bought our house was a blithe yuppie, and younger than my parents. He mentioned renovating, as if we wanted to hear it. I pictured him taking a sledgehammer to our vinyl couch. I was fifteen and had never moved before.

We stayed with my dad's folks in a Richmond neighborhood that had been full of middle-class black people, but then crack happened and the empty lots began to outnumber the schoolteachers and business owners. Aside from my dad, I'd never lived around black people. I wasn't allowed out at night. It didn't matter: I had nowhere to go.

I was angry at my parents for uprooting me and didn't consider how hard the move might have been for them—Dad probably facing sneers from neighbors who resented his leaving, then coming back with Mom, the palest person in a mile radius. She tried to put a happy face on things, but one morning, she was reading the paper in the dining room and told me that 62 percent of the high school students in Richmond were "at risk."

I asked, "At risk of what?"

She said, "Being homeless."

I imagined two-thirds of the kids at the school I was about to start dragging filthy sleeping bags through the hall, and raising their hands in class to ask for spare change. Then I said, "We're technically homeless."

She cast her eyes around the empty downstairs, then said, "No. We have somewhere to stay."

I was excited to go to a black high school because, finally, people wouldn't ask me about the black guy who dropped me off, or my kinky hair, or why I liked rap.

Instead, I was asked about the white lady who picked me up, and my red hair, and the rock music I liked. Sixty-two percent of my classmates did not seem homeless. I was the only skater except for this white professor's son that I made friends with, even if I knew it was a serious cop-out to only make friends with the white kid. I had no idea what anyone did after school.

I felt excluded from blackness, and like it was my fault that I couldn't fix it. But what was I gonna do? I had a lot to learn about taking scraps and making something beautiful and new. That's soul food. That's hip-hop.

 **FIVE** Oregon Hill was nine square blocks of run-down rowhouses between the college and the river. John Donahue and his little sister, Holly, were from there.

John Donahue was the first guy I heard get called a wigger. Holly Donahue was a year behind me. She had this rich red hair that the sun was catching through a classroom window on my first week of school in Richmond. It looked like ripe strawberries. It looked like ketchup in a new glass bottle. I kept looking. She saw me. I smiled. She didn't smile back.

I met John the next day when he hustled up to me in the locker room after PE, a short guy with pumped-up arms, holding a towel around his waist with his left hand and pushing my bare chest with the right, going, "'Choo lookin' at?" until I was sitting on the long wood bench in front of the lockers.

I didn't know who this guy was or what I'd been looking at. The other guys in the locker room were elbowing each other and throwing chins in our direction, getting excited for a fight. Then John shoved my forehead hard enough for the back of my head to bang a locker and said, "You ain't down with us. Keep away from my sister."

When my eyes focused again, I saw his red hair and cruel,

thin lips and put two and two together. He walked off, still holding his towel with one hand.

While I was trying not to cry, a guy I didn't know gave me a sly smile and nodded, mouthing, "Playa."

The last thing I felt like was a ladies' man, but I grinned so hard a tear squeezed from the outside corner of my left eye and stayed on my cheek until I snuck it away while taking off my gym shirt.

A week later, I was sitting in the lunchroom with the skater guy—the only white kid at school who wasn't from Oregon Hill. John was three tables over, holding a purse and running around the Oregon Hill table while this white girl with black-girl-style finger waves yelled, "Damn, boy! Give me that shit back!" in a way that made it clear she liked the attention.

The skater guy rolled his eyes and went, "Pssh. Wiggers."

And I went, "Wiggers?" picturing George Washington–style powdered wigs.

"Yeah," he scoffed.

"What you mean?" I asked.

John had stopped and was grinning, holding the purse behind him. The girl was reaching for it, strategically bumping him with her chest.

"It's a white person who acts black," my buddy said, then lowered his voice. "You put 'white' and the n-word together." He peered around the room to make sure no one had heard.

"Ha, I'm a wigger too," I said, and shoved the rest of my cheese sandwich in my mouth. I'd been experimenting with vegetarianism.

I was kinda pissed. A couple years before, when girls started touching my hair and asking, "What are you?" I'd tried to think of a word for black-and-white people like myself. I always thought "mulatto" sounded like a type of cookie, but "blight" and "wack" weren't working either. Leave it to the biggest dickhead at my school to get the name I'd been looking for.

Wigger.

Donahue was trying to act black, or an exaggerated version of it. Nothing like the black I experienced at home with my father. That's what would piss me off about Donahue, and other wiggers I encountered: their blackness was a cartoon put-on that ignored black dignity.

"You're not a wigger," mumbled my buddy.

"I've been looking for a name for me for a while," I said.

"Well, you don't *act* black," he said.

He probably thought John Donahue acted blacker than me.

"But I'm not white," I said.

"I guess."

SIX

My mom worked and my grandparents mall-walked in the afternoon. Bass would shake the porch as I walked up to my father's childhood home. He'd be inside, blasting new CDs by artists he'd liked in the '80s. At first, it felt like we were meeting halfway between grown-up and cool, and I'd never felt like either before.

Then one day I shut the bathroom door and a new Prince song was still louder than my peeing. I stood at the green sink, wanting to tell my father to turn it down. But if I told him to stop, then I couldn't play my music loud. I thought about how, for me, the point of loud music was to have someone tell you to turn it down, and now he couldn't tell me to do that. So I went up to my room and shut that door, too.

There were things that I didn't trust my middle-aged parents to explain, so I was glad when Lucius came along that first fall in Richmond. I'd just been called "Afro Puffs," because of my big hair, and it made me feel like my entire life was a joke that I wasn't in on. I went to the bathroom across from the nurse's office—the only boys' room in the school where the stalls had doors—and shut myself in one, just to be alone.

Suddenly, this bulky dude with chubby cheeks poked his head under the door and went, "Yo, man. You chief?"

I put my hands over my crotch and scowled at him. "What the hell? Get out of here, man. This stall is occupied."

I expected the guy to go, "He said, 'occupied,'" to whatever goons were out there with him, but instead he reached an arm under the door and pointed at me, "Naw, you chief, money?"

"No, I'm not Chief Money." I pulled a stank face and waved my hand. "Go on!"

I lifted a foot to push his face away and he grabbed the sole of my sneaker.

"Naw." He clapped my foot back onto the floor. "Do. You. Chief. The. Peace. Pipe?"

With each word he put a thumb and pointer to his mouth, in the universal sign for weed smoking.

"Ohhh." I smiled and we nodded at the same time. "Why do you wanna know?" I asked.

"Hey. If you do, find me when you get off the bus after school. My name Lucius."

With that, he disappeared.

I wanted to know what clique Lucius might get me into, but didn't see him swaggering slowly through the halls with the football players, leaning on a locker flirting with girls, or shouting songs off the radio in the press of people going out the door after the last bell. Then, when I got off the bus that afternoon, he was on a green park bench across the street, giving me a nod and a low Black Power fist. I returned the nod and crossed the street to join him, feeling a rush of excitement as I placed a foot on the bench itself and lifted myself to sit on its back, like Lucius.

"Thought I'd seen you 'round here," he said.

"Yeah, I stay a couple blocks over."

"Cool. Everyone else here is either running the streets or too dang old. Glad we got some new blood." He rolled his head up to meet my eye. "You ain't runnin' the streets, is you?"

He was around my age, but seemed wise, and moved like he was up to his neck in mud.

"Naw," I said.

"You sound different, where you from?" he asked, delicately patting the pockets of his baggy jeans.

"DC."

"You like go-go?" he asked.

"It's all right."

"Yeah. Just a'ight." He drummed a swinging go-go beat on his thighs and sang, "Doin' the butt."

I joined him to go, "Pretty prett-ay," and we chuckled.

"Chocolate City," he declared.

"Mmm-hmm," I answered, not admitting that we'd lived almost twenty miles out.

"You look more like a fudge ripple, vanilla swirl type cat, though," he said.

"You got me."

"But I know there's some soul in there." He flicked his pointer finger at my chest and I saw that he was palming a blunt. "Let's chief, money."

I thought we'd go deeper into the park but he lit up right there on the back of the bench, and after a hit, I stopped being paranoid that my pop would drive by.

Cut to a montage of Lucius playing me the song "Afro Puffs" so I got the joke, practicing elaborate handshakes with me, pacing my bedroom while we perfected our bops, and us bobbing our heads in unison to hip-hop tapes. It was a lot of work, but I was blacking up real nice.

Then the skater kid took me to a punk show in a smoky, shoebox-size nightclub where everything was painted black.

Anything that sounded like a skateboard thwacking pavement before flying got my attention, so I was into the first band. The empty semicircle in front of the stage told me I was the only one.

I liked the wide way the bassist planted his feet, then looked from the drummer to the guitarists like he was anchoring them all. My mind wandered to the beat-up guitar case I'd carried into our storage space during the move. Then my friend slapped my back and pointed out other skaters he knew, and people from bands I'd never heard of, and a guy with a blond beard and hair below his ears who'd just got out of jail. I wondered where all these people went when they weren't there.

When the second band started, everyone else stepped up to the stage. From the back near the bar, I saw buzz-cut heads and oval skate shoes popping up from the crowd. The people under them made mushroom stems of their arms and passed them around before the stems collapsed and the crowd surfers were swallowed again.

With the music in the club louder than my dad's stereo, I couldn't feel the worry that was always reverberating off my folks. I didn't stress about if I looked geeky when I ran up to crowd-surf. I didn't hesitate when I grabbed two strangers' shoulders and pushed up. And as hands pressed my back, calves, and ticklish sides as they passed me around above the crowd, I forgot everything else. I wasn't a skater. I wasn't black. I was someone new with louder music. And I didn't have to try too hard to do it.

I got my dad's old bass out of storage and would play it unplugged on my bed into the night, finding staccato rhythms then easy notes. A couple months after I started trying to forget that I was black, I joined my first punk band. Lucius would come to shows with me and linger in the back, remembering the heavy mosh parts, lighting up at the occasional rap lyric shouted into the mic between songs, asking why people don't fight when they do that dance where they hit each other, and tailing kids between bands, imitating their walks and gestures, their every movement a hilarious antithesis to his cool demeanor.

I started seeing less of Lucius, but when our paths crossed, he would clown me for trying to sidestep race. My Black Card would burn my ass through my wallet, where it rubbed against the family photo I used to prove I was black, its corners rounding, its faces scuffing to a blur.

 **SEVEN** I'd dropped out of college almost two years before because playing music with my friends made me feel like I was making my own world, and homework never did. Right before Mona got hired, Paper Fire did a kinda awesome but mainly pointless monthlong tour around the States. It was my first time in California, and I came home five hundred dollars poorer. Ever since, I'd been getting this feeling like punk was a quick fix, but life wasn't that quick.

On my first shift after that tour, I made a latte for a yuppie I remembered from Freshman English. She smiled and tucked a buck in the tip jar, and I felt like I was stuck on a dock, waving goodbye to a cruise ship, so I made a deal with myself to start saying yes to whatever opportunities came up.

At closing, that hippie Nesta asked me if I wanted to go to his friend's place to "bitch-slap a few brain cells."

"Does that mean weed?" I asked.

"No diggity, man," he said as I kept on cringing. "His pad's pretty near here. Let's go after I get done mopping."

I decided this counted as an opportunity.

You'd think that the promise of weed would have lit a fire under Nesta's ass, but he still took forever with the floor, doing this annoying little bunny hop dance to the noodly CD he'd put on.

Twenty minutes later, I left my bike locked in front of the café and hopped in Nesta's station wagon, which smelled like wet dog and Nag Champa. Taking the four-way stops at a roll, he drove us a mile north to the Devil's Triangle neighborhood.

His buddy lived in a rickety four-flat, a block up Park Avenue from the pool hall where the manager told Russell, "The only people we don't allow in here are assholes and niggers, and I can only be sure you're not one of the two."

I forget Nesta's friend's name, but he was a college-aged white guy who wore circular metal glasses and a fistful of goatee. He sprawled on a beanbag chair, exposing thick shadows of dirt on the soles of his bare feet. Above him hung a huge black-and-white poster of a jazz trumpet player in a suit.

First, he got me high, passing me a heavy purple glass bong, which I propped on my thighs and hit on the couch while he nodded slow approval and Nesta slapped my shoulder going, "It's dank as hell, right?"

Just as I was forgetting to breathe and realizing that I'd smoked way more than usual, Nesta told his pal, "Hey, he's in a band."

His voice echoed as if from far away.

"You play guitar?" the weedman asked.

"A bit," I croaked, and an acoustic appeared in my hand.

Moments later, we were all grinning stupidly as I picked out single-string bass lines on the guitar, Nesta hit his palm with a maraca, and his friend tapped out a hip-hop beat on an hourglass-shaped African drum. The weed silenced my inner punk rocker, who would have clowned our jam session endlessly, and I lost myself in the groove, feeling like I was doing something deliciously surreptitious, cheating on the serious, thrashing music my friends and I based our lives around.

The weedman slowed the beat down to something more driving and, as I vamped on an open string, trying to catch the new rhythm, Nesta crowed, "Yeah! Is that 'So Fresh and So Clean Clean?'"

The weedman said, "You know it, brotha."

At "brotha," I went back to dying the death that had begun when Nesta said "no diggity," then asked, "What's 'So Fresh and So Clean Clean'?"

All hippie percussion clattered to a stop as they gawked at me in amazement. The weedman said, "Dude. Outkast?"

"Oh, OK." I nodded. I knew that name.

"You know Outkast, right?" Nesta asked. "Dude, put it on!" he shouted at his friend.

Ever stumble across the perfect thing that you had no idea you were looking for? That's how I felt when Outkast came on. Fast and fun rapping, plus my father's out-there psychedelic black rock music, and a purple wave of funk, all crashed across my stoned body as I sat grinning on that couch.

The problem was, the weedman wouldn't shut up about it.

"It's like perfect southern music," he pontificated. "It just, like, makes me want to sit on the porch and eat chicken."

He curled back his lips and held an invisible drumstick to his mouth.

"Wait, what? Why?" I asked, getting that feeling like what I'd heard was racist, but I couldn't prove it.

"Because it sounds like the south." He unfolded an arm and pointed it at the tall speaker on the floor to his right.

"OK?"

"And that's what we do here!" He grinned.

Outkast created a buffer zone between me and the white idiots I was getting high with, but I was still antsy and irritated. I kept sneaking glances out the balcony door, at the identical building across the street. Soon enough, I abruptly stood, thanked them both, took a look at the CD cover, where two long-haired black dudes posed in front of a black-and-white American flag, and walked to the record store, where I blew half the day's tips on a used copy of the album.

I love hip-hop because it's courage and bluster in the face of a world it can't control. Try explaining that to a white person who is hung up on the lyrics about guns and bitches. I don't love those lyrics either, and really had to think it through, but decided that the offensive side of rap is a symptom of the disease we got from white people. Hip-hop in your head is a gun in your pocket: it makes you feel like no one can fuck with you, and I needed that right then.

STATUE OF
ROBERT E. LEE

 **ONE** Black Guys I Want to Be

Big guy who works the grill at a cookout and wears an apron that says "Kiss the Cook." He isn't a jerk about grilling, just talks a little smack, cooks meat with fire, and keeps kids from coming too close to the hot grill.

Halves guy who has one side of his hair braided, the other blown out, and one sweatpant leg up showing white tube sock. He wiggles the leg with the pants down while he's sitting on the bus, so it looks like he's trying to get that pant leg to inch up and join the other.

Serious writer guy who looks uncomfortable in the suit he's wearing for his author photo, and needs to ash his cigarette.

High school guy with a ball of toilet paper in his runny nose like what.

Motorcycle guy in a denim vest with a cool biker gang name on it like Jackson Ward Black Dragons, who is the reason his mother keeps plastic on the couch.

Jazz drummer guy who stays expressionless behind the kit, transferring all of his sweat to the white folks in the audience.

Leather vest no shirt beaded headband guy.

Wife made him go to church so he made her go to Ribbit's for fish and mimosas guy.

I wish I was awesomer. I wish I was blacker. I wish I could just settle into something and be it.

TWO

There are only first impressions in Richmond. No one calls the Italian place at Strawberry and Main "Bernetti's." They call it "the old Vibe Café," because that's the business that used to be there. And no one eats at the old Vibe Café, because meals cost more than ten bucks.

That "new thing in an old building" line of thought applies to people as well, so I'm sure that someone would call me "the old punk rock coffee-shop guy" if I went out and really tried to do black stuff—going to the nightclub at Broad and Harrison on Friday nights, wearing baggy jeans, whatever.

If the city is full of flags supporting an army that lost over a century ago, it's not gonna forget who you were last year.

Mona didn't know me last year. We'd never even met before her first shift. She was in the dorms while I was at a house show a couple blocks away. Her folks were helping her rent an apartment while I was cramming my life into milk crates and moving into the farmhouse.

It's like we'd been living in different planes of the same universe. That was the problem with my punk rock life: it was super limiting, and I'd missed out on a lot more than just black people touchpoints. I'd missed women like Mona and simple conversation equalizers like pop culture and sports.

Even better than not being stuck in the past, Mona's looking forward. A couple shifts in, I was back-flushing the espresso machine. She passed behind me carrying some muffin trays, stopped, and asked, "What's your major anyway?"

"It was English," I said.

"What is it now?" She watched me as she walked into the oven room in back.

"I stopped going a couple years ago."

I looked back down at the machine right as a little fountain of hot, soap-slick water sprayed out and burned between my thumb and forefinger. I was shaking my hand when Mona walked back out. I didn't want to hear about how I was ruining my future, or find a nice way to tell her that I'd showed up after winter break and everyone on campus was talking on new cell phones and I felt like they were creating a future that I wanted no part of, so I asked, "What's your major?"

"International Relations," she said, and I swear she stood up taller as she said it and it didn't annoy the shit out of me.

I wrapped the front of my apron around my hand, squeezed, and asked, "What do you do with that?"

"Maybe work in government. I'm trying to get an internship in DC."

The closest anyone I knew came to that was when one of Russell's roommates moved up to DC to apprentice at a tattoo shop.

"That'd be cool."

She smiled and turned to help a customer.

While my burnt hand throbbed, I cleaned the espresso

machine and thought about how I'd work in kitchens to pay the rent between band tours, but Mona would probably stop having jobs like this when she graduated. A few years later, she might be on her second glass of wine at a dinner party, talking about this wild coffee shop she'd worked at in college. I'd still be wild at a coffee shop.

THREE

Russell and I nicknamed all of the coffee shop regulars. Most are named after their orders. For example, Russell had a crush on Skim Milk, a shy blond yuppie who looked great in pink. Small Coffee tipped his one-cent change. Soy Latte left his drink on the milk bar while he blew up the bathroom. Ham was in an ad for the Japanese steakhouse where they cooked at your table. Tea with Lemon was a guitar teacher with a million classic rock T-shirts. Laptop didn't drink her computer, but you get the idea.

"Here comes Three-Piece Tarik!"

Mona'd been getting in on the game. The man himself was gliding across the patio like butter on a hot pan. Tarik was too mysterious to have a regular order, so he was named after the fancy men's clothing store he owned. He was one of our few black customers. I watched him closely for pointers, wishing my closet full of thrift store western shirts and tight jeans would transform into the type of clothes he wore: linen pants, and blazers for all weather. Wishing I wasn't wound so tight and could convey that much feeling with a nod and a "My brother" like he gave me at the counter, hand outstretched for a fist-squeeze handshake.

I lit up a little bit when he called me "brother." I've even caught Lucius adding a Three-Piece Tarik–ish roll to his walk, moving like a funky Rube Goldberg device, his center driving forward with purpose, each limb playing a different drum.

He greeted Mona with another nod and an approving, friendly grumble, more sound than word.

She said "Hey" back.

I took up space between the counter and espresso machine, wanting to listen, wanting to join in.

"Coffee today?" I asked, then worried he'd think I was trying to rush him out.

"Yeah," he said slowly, with the nod to match it.

I cut behind Mona and poured light roast into a blue mug that set off Tarik's pink oxford shirt. Mona's rootsy soul CD ended and some slick mall punk came on, that Russell and I played at work because it didn't have screaming. I cringed at the dentist's drill guitar and the singer's first nasal note as I sat the coffee on the counter.

Tarik had a way of looking surprised, where he slowly drew up to full height and gazed in silence for a moment before exhaling and sinking back into his catlike hunch. He did that at the musical transition then told Mona, "Hey, I tried that sushi place."

"Oh, did you like it?" Mona rang in the coffee with her left hand.

"Yeah," Tarik said. "Especially the California roll."

Being around him, I felt blacker by proximity, until I thought about it too hard and wondered at weird, small stuff, like what he ate for breakfast and if I had the same English muffins, would it make me blacker?

"What's in a California roll?" I asked, thinking of the huge burritos Paper Fire ate on tour in San Francisco.

"You never had one?" Mona asked. "It's got avocados in it. It's a good one to start with."

"Oh, OK." I nodded, a little embarrassed, and retreated to the kitchen, where I went back to scooping cream cheese into little plastic cups, a task that always ends with sticky hands. Not eating sushi would've earned me black points from Lucius, but it set me apart from Mona and Tarik.

It was the tail end of the shift, quiet before lunch. Coffee beans were portioned and ground. I was staring into the middle distance above the patio, seeing a whole lotta nothing, dreaming up black people coffee drinks that'd get me back into Lucius's good graces. Cognac mocha. Blacker'n a mug coffee. Sweet tea latte. There was a coconut shampoo smell and a smack on my upper arm. Mona. Perfectly familiar.

"Hey." She put an elbow on the counter and shook her head. "You've really never had sushi?"

I smiled, sheepish, and said, "Yeah."

We had a lot of chicken and mac 'n' cheese growing up. Chinese takeout was as foreign as we got.

"Well, look," Mona said. "We've got some nori at my place. You wanna come by? I could make some tonight."

Oh snap. Oh snap. Oh snap.

"Yeah. Yeah." I nodded. Then kept nodding. Then felt stupid and stopped. "What time you thinking?"

"Say seven?"

I'll always remember the way she flicked her wrist and

spread the fingers on her left hand, as if she were waving the seven into the air, so everyone could see we were about to hang out.

"Seven's cool." I didn't nod this time. "What's nori, anyway?"

FOUR

Mason and I were sharing the bottom floor of a house off Boulevard, this main drag that stretches from beautiful Byrd Park to the bus station in a little over two miles. Our pointy-roofed building looked like a farmhouse, with white shingles, four windows facing the street, and a horseshoe-shaped porch with a set-back front door.

I found the apartment through a coffee shop regular who heard me complaining about my old roommates' late-night guitar jams, and said I should take over her lease when she moved in with her boyfriend. The landlord never upped the rent, so Mason and I each paid $220 a month. He got the big room in front, and let me keep a lot of my stuff in the living room, while I slept in the tiny room under the stairs to the second-floor apartment.

I appreciated every square inch of our apartment because it was the first time I hadn't just been renting a room in a punk house with someone and their partner living in each room, and a bathroom you had to wear shoes in. We had show flyers, a couple Painting 101 splatterfests on the walls, thrift store furniture, and wicked drafts by the windows, but it felt good to be able to spread my stuff out, and almost never find some dumbasses drinking on the couch when I wanted to be alone.

Mason was a little too anal for me to ever want to hang out with him, but that also meant he did his dishes. He made for a good roommate, especially since he never slept there, but it was also kinda weird. We'd been in a band together for over a year and I felt like I hardly knew the guy. Still, I was sure that his vegetarian ass wouldn't appreciate the fact that Lucius was using his spatula to fry bologna.

After work, I followed the greasy, salty smell into the kitchen, where I found Lucius at the range, smoke arcing around his bulky shoulders and disappearing in front of the Band-Aid-colored walls.

When we moved in, I stayed up all night before going paint shopping. What seemed like a pleasant toast brown in the hardware store dried pink. It was like cooking inside a giant piece of bubblegum.

I coughed and said, "Aye, man."

Lucius looked up, the back of his black durag touching the strap of his A-shirt. "'Sup."

"Mason's gonna be pissed if he knows you're cooking meat with his spatula," I said. "And it smells."

Lucius held up the spatula and bugged his eyes incredulously while grease dripped off it. "Dang," he said slowly. "Looks like I better wash it, then."

"Don't forget," I said.

"And if this smell so nasty, you ain't gotta eat any."

The spatula dinged into the skillet then emerged carrying a glistening disc of pink meat, which Lucius slapped on a slice of mayo-slathered white bread.

"But, hey," I said. "I'm hungry. And you know the rules, if you're coming in here cooking, you're sharing."

"Aye, bruh," Lucius said. "There's four pieces of bread on this plate, ain't there? I'll even forget you insulted my cooking."

"My man."

"Ain't your man." He turned from the stove and bucked at me. A drop of grease landed on the tiles between us.

Lucius and I took our sandwiches into the living room and sat perpendicular, me on the couch—this puffy neon floral thing that the old tenant had left behind—and Lucius on the love seat, while an old soul record spun on the turntable that blocked the broken fireplace, the singer's horny yowl cranking up the urgency of the night to come.

Lucius wiped his mouth with the back of his hand and said, "This is a big one tonight, bruh."

"Thanks for reminding me."

The bite of sandwich felt wide and hot in my chest. I was beyond "going to a girl's house" nervous. "Going to a black woman's apartment for what might be a date" had piled on top and I kept forgetting to breathe.

"How am I supposed to act?" I asked.

"Like you always do around girls." Lucius slid his sandwich across his plate, leaving a slug trail of grease. "Get so scared of acting like a creep that you sit back, don't do nothing, and look kinda creepy in the process."

"But what if I wanna do something?"

"Then do something." He shrugged and took another bite.

I sighed and leaned back, plate tilting in my lap. "Do I do anything different because she's black?"

"Yeah, dawg. Tap dance." He laughed into the top of his fist.

"Shut up."

His stomach wobbled with laughter. Finally, he wiped away a tear and said, "A real brotha would let her fix him a plate. And not help with the dishes."

"Man, you know I'm not with that 'a woman's place is in the kitchen' stuff."

"And look where that got you."

"A date with a 'sista.'" I picked my sandwich back up, remembering to feel happy about this.

"A true sista wouldn't have invited your corny ass by." He swatted the air. "Or made sushi."

"Maybe this isn't some 'real brotha, real sista' stuff," I said. "Maybe she likes me. We get along."

Lucius screwed up the left side of his mouth and raised the eyebrow above it, the best way to say "nigga, please" without making a sound.

"Fine," I went on. "I'm going in alone. I don't need you standing over me, telling me to jiggle her ass while she's cooking."

"Your boy Russell would like that," Lucius pointed out.

I rolled my eyes.

"You don't want me to coach you on how to dance to something smooth?" he asked.

"She likes Phish," I moaned.

"I do, too," he said.

"Nah, like the band," I said.

His face was blank.

"It's hippie music, Lucius."

"Figures." He shook his head and looked at his sandwich like it was the only normal thing in the room.

"Hey!" I felt bold after telling him to stay home, and started counting off on my fingers. "A date with a black woman that I don't just like because she's black, checking Russell on the proper way for white folks to rap along to the radio . . . this is the type of stuff that gets a man his Black Card."

"You're not getting it back quite yet, Brokely Carmichael," Lucius said, and tapped his right pocket. I stared, halfway to leaping for it. He caught me looking, frowned, and swept his hand to the arm of the couch.

"What do I need to do to get it back?" I asked. "I'm supposed to move to Church Hill or something?"

He looked me in the eye before saying, "I can't tell you. You'll know when you do it."

I stood up, paced to Mason's bedroom door. "Man, I can't win. You have people checking you like this all this time?"

"Don't you worry about that." He pointed his sandwich at me, bit into a gun shape. "I don't need your advice. Now sit your ass down and eat. Gotta sustain yourself before you eat that sushi nonsense."

FIVE

From: Russell
4:17 pm
got vodka an pindapple soda ldts drink

To: Russell
4:22 pm
cant. Plans.

From: Russell
4:28 pm
shutup. Cme over

To: Russell
4:30 pm
At monas

From: Russell
4:30 pm
wut!

Mona lived a mile or so away in the Fan District. The neighborhood name is literal: the streets fan out going west from the college, with new avenues branching off from the middle of residential blocks, and triangular concrete parks filling the spaces where the alleys run wide.

The Fan is beautiful and haphazard and contains two types of century-old row houses: fancy historical places, and run-down joints that are sectioned into student apartments. The historical homes have plaques with Confederate General Robert E. Lee's silhouette, and the student pads have overflowing recycling bins on their porches, hobo signals for party animals and the people who call the cops on them.

I pedaled through the neighborhood to Mona's, breeze drying the sweat that started after my shower, as more sweat took its place. I lifted my elbows to coast through a stop sign, the sky a little river running above tree-lined Floyd Avenue. What would her place look like? I'd been in parents' houses, grandparents' houses, but never a black person's college apartment. I'd only met white people through punk, so that door had closed when I was still in high school.

———

Mona was sitting on her porch's top step, bare knees spread in a carefree way, talking on a cordless phone and turning a small key ring in her left hand. She'd leave those keys on the steel shelf above the dish sink at work. I'd soap mugs and think about how I respected that key ring because it was simple: just her black car key, a couple house keys, and a flat metal mushroom pendant for a touch of groovy flair. I remember girly girls at school waving around elaborate webs of key chain with miniature stuffed animals and World's Best Daughter medallions dangling off them. It always seemed like a cry for attention. That's not Mona's style, and I like that.

As I plunked a sneaker on the bottom step she said, "OK, Mom. Love you, too," and clicked the phone off.

"Hey, nice key chain," I said because I am always smooth.

"Uh, thanks," she said as she stood up. "Come on in."

She turned and stepped toward the door. I said, "This is nice," and sorta meant the fresh-painted white porch and sorta meant the view of her round butt under her cutoffs.

She said, "Yeah, I'm glad we got this place."

Somewhere, Lucius was nodding and scratching his goatee with my Black Card, updating his "Respect our African queens . . . and those white girls you tend to mess around with" speech for tonight.

Inside, Mona's building looked like the once-grand house that it was, with newer walls dividing apartments, and the Fan's patented must of cigarettes and old wood blanketing me when I walked in.

Mona opened a door to the left of a wide staircase and we passed into her high-ceilinged living room, where still summer heat stretched from the scarred wood floor to the tarnished ceiling light. Tension hummed through my body, threatening to send my hands waving, my feet in opposite directions.

Was my voice deep and cool when I thanked her for holding the door?

Was I walking into her living room all stiff like a white guy?

Why couldn't I be myself?

Who was I?

I've been so many people that I like to wait and see what the situation calls for, but I couldn't do that if I was trying to get back my card. I couldn't wait. I had to be black.

We hung out on some stools in the kitchen and rolled our own sushi, which was basically a burrito with a big leaf of seaweed instead of a tortilla. Rice tumbled out the bottom of mine when I took my first bite.

"I'm new to this!" I said when Mona laughed.

"I can tell."

"Shit, you got a fork?" I asked.

"You'd pick that rice up with your hand if you were alone, wouldn't you?" she asked.

"I'm not alone," I said.

Her knee brushed mine as she got off her stool, the second time that night. The beer put an extra bounce in her stride as she walked around the kitchen island, throwing three fingers in the air and saying, "So, three packs of D batteries, and there was so much bottled water in the trunk that I had to put my bag in the back seat . . . then he made me carry it into the rest stop when we got lunch!"

"Why?" I asked.

"In case someone broke into the car and took my Strawberry Shortcake duffel bag." She shook her head and chuckled into the silverware drawer.

"Man, camping is supposed to be relaxing, but it stresses me out, too."

"My dad was beyond stressed," she said, walking back around. "I think he sat on a log the whole night. That was my last year doing Brownies."

"My dad would have done the same."

Black people common ground.

We ate, quiet for the first time in a while, then she pushed her plate aside and said, "Wanna go in the living room?"

"Sure. You don't want any help with dishes or anything?"

"Nah. You aren't as uncouth as you look, you know that?" she said.

We carried our beers by the cans' top rims and moved into the living room. It had white walls and a mix of hard-looking antique furniture and hippie staples like batik pillows and a wall hanging with crocheted mushrooms. I hoped she'd sit on the couch and pat the cushion next to her but she collapsed into a round, one-person papasan chair.

There was this dude at my high school who'd flirt in this joking/not joking way where he'd throw his wallet on the floor in the middle of class, say, "Oh, I dropped my wallet. Let me get it," then bend over and point his ass at a girl, who would make a big show out of not looking.

I wanted to test the waters with Mona by doing something jokey but retractable like that, so I bent hard at the waist and spun my butt in her direction as I went to sit on the velvety pink couch. But I miscalculated my spin and hit my tailbone on the couch's hard arm. I grunted as I tumbled to my right, landing sideways on the cushions. Somewhere, Lucius laughed and coughed.

"Sorry 'bout that," I said, and righted myself.

"No biggie," she said. "You OK?"

"Yeah," I nodded, thinking I should have laughed.

We were three feet apart with a floor plant in a wicker basket nudging into the space between us.

She pointed at the couch I'd been hell-bent on breaking. "Hey, we have a new couch."

I smoothed my hand across the thin cushion and said, "Cool. Vintage?"

"I guess so." She smiled. "From Bree's grandmother's house."

Her roommate Bree is a white girl who always looks like she'd rather be in a rocking chair, knitting.

"Oh," I said. "Did her grandma pass?"

Mona nodded.

"That's lousy. I'm sorry." I sipped beer and, before I could check myself, turned my head and took a whiff of the couch, caught myself mid-sniff, and said, "Well, it doesn't smell like old lady."

Mona smiled. At my dead grandma comment. Wow.

"You sure?" she asked. "Maybe you should sniff my couch again to check."

I could practically hear Lucius bellowing, "Girl, come over here and let me sniff *yo'* couch!"

I laughed through my nose, embarrassed. She laughed too and my embarrassment melted.

"I guess I just know my grandma's old lady smell," I said. "She had a whole mess of perfumes and hair products on her dresser and you could smell them out in the hall."

She nodded like she was having a similar memory then asked, "Did your grandma sit on this couch?"

I wiggled my nose. "Not that I can tell. It's a cool couch, though. Hey, you ever notice there aren't any rap songs about antiques?"

Mona was leaning forward, pulling the lid off this colorful tin on the coffee table. She sat back and twirled it between her hands so the ceiling light flashed off of it.

"I guess there aren't," she said. "How'd you think of that?"

"I was thinking about how sometimes old stuff is cool, but thought it might sound stupid to be sitting here and saying your couch has 'character' or something."

"It does, though," she said, and pointed an open hand at the couch like she was presenting it. "When was the last time you saw a pink couch?"

"Never. I feel like I'm chillin' on a tongue."

She laughed and pulled a pipe and plastic baggie out of the

tin, then said, "I was gonna offer you some of this, but you already sound high."

Her fingernails had chipped sky-blue nail polish and she used them to break up the weed on the back of a magazine.

"Is that the litmus test?" she asked. "Something's not cool if it's not in a rap song?"

"It's a start. We should make a rap song about lattes and pink couches, just to keep outta trouble."

She rolled the magazine into a chute and tapped one end, sending the last of the crumbled weed into the pipe.

"Do you ever catch crap for being different?" I asked.

"Not lately. High school ended a while ago."

"What happened then?" I asked. "Sorry if I sound like a shrink."

She waved a hand. "No, nothing much. That just seems like the time when people are extra worried about fitting in."

"Lucky you for getting over that."

"Well, you, too." She sipped her beer.

"Oh. Really?"

"You seem like someone who does his own thing," she said. "That's not easy but it's cool."

"You, too," I said then lifted my beer, "Uh, cheers!"

We tapped our cans together and I should have stopped but I had to know so I said, "But you're black."

She nodded slow like *Yeah, no kidding.*

I said, "And you have a lot of white friends. And you just said 'litmus test,' and I wish I knew more people who weren't scared to say smart shit like that."

She swept her fingers across her palm for stray bits of weed and said, "So what? You think Bree and all them make black jokes at me or something?"

She shook her head like it was out of the question then said, "My friends are my friends. They wouldn't do that."

"They never do, like, 'just kidding' jokes?"

"Nah," she said.

I was quiet while she turned and sat up in her chair to hit play on the stereo behind her. Brassy jazz began.

When she settled back down, I said, "How about black people?"

"What about black people?"

"Do you catch crap for not being black enough?" Being "black enough" had been hanging over my head for years, but this was the first time I'd said those two words out loud.

"Once again," she said. "My friends are my friends, the black ones and the white ones."

"You're lucky," I said.

With one hand, she picked up a swirly glass pipe and a plastic lighter with a gold star sticker like teachers used to give out. "Here. Smoke."

I started swaying in my seat to the jazz's lurching rhythm, then felt self-conscious in front of Mona. Black people are supposed to be good dancers. I like to dance drunk at parties or alone in the bathroom, but I don't know if I'm any good. Lucius gives me a nod and a smile when I dance, but he might just be encouraging me. And when he dances, it seems natural. The humping isn't exaggerated. His shoulders have a life of their own. I don't feel natural because whenever I'm doing it, I start wondering how I look. If I dance good. If I dance good because I'm black. Or if I dance good for a white guy. Or if I dance plain ol' bad but look good to white folks who expect me to be a good dancer because I'm black.

The weed tasted piney and sharp. I coughed a mushroom cloud toward an old-fashioned metal floor lamp. My brain was a porch light. My smile was lazy.

"Dang."

Mona laughed and took the bowl. "Dang is right."

"Where do you get that?" I asked. It was way better than the stuff I got from Russell's metalhead roommate.

"One of Bree's friends."

"Does Bree hang out with a lot of black people?"

"I mean, her roommate's black." Mona pointed at herself. "And she knows my friends."

"This might sound weird—"

Mona sputtered out a laugh.

"What?" I asked.

"The guy who's hanging out on a tongue just warned me he might say something weird."

I thumped the couch and laughed. "You're right."

"Well, what might sound weird?" she asked.

"If you meet a white person can you kinda sense if they hang out with black people?"

"Hmm." She sat back and frowned. "You don't mean like when you see a white kid wearing FUBU and using all the slang?"

"No, I mean, sometimes there are little clues, like if a white dude's beard is extra lined-up . . ."

She pointed at me and said, "Or a white girl has a booty and seems cool with it!"

I laughed, embarrassed.

"Well, sure, but what about Bree?" I asked.

"Leave my roommate's booty out of this."

"I am. For real. I mean, Bree seems super white."

"Yeah, but where I grew up is super white. Just because a white person didn't see *Poetic Justice* or something doesn't mean that they're racist. You know? If someone's cool, they treat you well."

"True." I nodded. "You want another beer?"

"Sure. They're in the crisper."

I closed my eyes and took a few deep breaths with my head in the cool fridge, then walked back to the living room with a can in each hand. When I held one out to Mona, she looked up fast like she'd forgotten I was there. If she was Russell, I would have made a joke about how high she looked, but this felt different. When my friends and I smoke, it's a race. The finish line? Us bloated with corn chips and too high to talk. With Mona, smoking was something we did during lulls in the conversation.

I sat down and asked, "Did you always have, like, a hippie style?"

After a sip, she said, "That was pretty much my teenage phase."

"I bet you were cool."

"Definitely not cool," she said with a smile. "There was one hippie store in town and it was such a big deal when my friend's mom drove us there in eighth grade." She leaned forward to pick up the bowl again. "I remember I got this tie-dye shirt with a bunch of mushrooms on it and had to pretend like I didn't know what the mushrooms meant when I brought it home."

We both laughed.

"You get to keep it?" I asked.

"Oh, yeah." She smiled. "The next time we had pizza, my mom ordered one with mushrooms on it. And I hate mushrooms! After that, she called it my 'pizza shirt.' I still have it."

She pointed toward her bedroom, which was through a tall sliding door at the front of the apartment, and I imagined it folded in her childhood dresser.

"See, you were cool," I said.

"But not, like, *cool*. I wasn't popular."

"Duh," I said as I sipped my beer.

She paused with the bowl a couple inches from her mouth. "What's that supposed to mean?"

"There's no way you were a stuck-up, popular kid," I said. "That's why you were cool. I bet we would have gotten along."

Lucius nodded approval at me not saying "been friends," because that would have implied that friendship was all I was there for.

She dropped her shoulders and her guard, took another hit, then said, "I dunno. You might have been too busy being a cool band dude."

When black people call me "dude," I worry they're making fun of me for being part white.

"Who ever said my band was cool?"

I watched her face, waiting for her to look up from the

lighter, meet my eyes and not lose them. Instead she turned the stereo down a bit then asked, "Don't you guys have a concert soon?"

"Yeah. Tomorrow night. At a house in Jackson Ward."

"Cool." She smiled. "So it's like a party?"

I nodded and shrugged.

She said, "Maybe Bree and I will come."

"That'd be nice. Don't feel like you have to come, though. I'm scared it's gonna suck for some reason."

"If you and Russell have a band, I kinda need to see this," she said.

The tough part about making friends with people who aren't punk is when they want to come see your band, and you're scared they're going to hate the late start, screaming noise, and dark, dank venue. You don't want them to feel obligated to come, but you don't want them to feel like you think they're not cool enough to go.

Our fingers touched when she handed me the weed, and I decided that I was all in. I'd pass her beers and see to it she had fun, and make sure Russell didn't talk to her too much or ask if I'd put it in her ass.

"You should come. We'll hang out."

"Was punk rock always your thing?" she asked me.

"I started liking it in high school. I mainly liked hip-hop before that. I don't know if it was a teenage phase or what."

It was hitting me that punk is a stronger identity than hippie. Like, if you're punk, it becomes a compass for your life. If something's not punk, you don't do it, or you make a big deal out of how wack it is when you do it. If you're hippie, you just wear earth tones and get some Buddhist-looking stuff for your apartment, but you can still go out into the world without acting like you're at war with it. You can enjoy things without feeling guilty.

"Punks don't like hippies, do they?" she asked.

"I guess not," I said, and squashed the impulse to do a Hookah Guy impression. "I don't care, though. My mom was a hippie."

"Well, you're not really punk," she said. "You don't have a mohawk and stuff."

"Well, you're not really black," I said.

I was trying to joke but Mona sat forward in her chair and knit her face up and I expected her to say something snappy back but she just glared at me.

After I hoped Lucius would be proud of me for pulling rank and calling someone out for not being black, I felt like a fool and started stammering, "Well, I meant that, uh, like, I was jok—uh, like I feel like I keep getting told stuff like that and maybe you'd relate because you're different too and we could joke about—"

"Look, man." Mona pointed at her face and wagged her finger up and down. "If this isn't black, I don't know what is."

"You're right," I said, fast. "I'm sorry."

"It's . . ." She paused and sat back in her chair. "Why do you keep asking me all these questions?"

The beer and the cream cheese we'd put in the sushi, and the salty, living taste of the seaweed bubbled in my stomach. It was my turn to sit forward and put an elbow on my knee and my forehead in my hand.

"I always feel pulled between worlds. And I wondered if you ever did, too. Because you're cool and different but you seem so . . ." I paused. "Comfortable."

"You don't get to talk to black people very much, do you?" she asked.

"No."

"Have you ever dated a black girl?"

"Do mixed girls count?"

"I don't know, do they?"

I pictured Lucius using my Black Card to jimmy the lock on his grandma's liquor cabinet, snapping the card by mistake, then just shrugging it off.

"Look." Mona clapped her hands on her knees. "That 'really black' stuff is . . . wrong. There isn't one way to be black. Everyone who is black is black. Even mixed nuts like you."

She sat back in the chair, triumphant from her joke. I bit my tongue and laughed, glad that she'd broken the tension, even at my expense.

"'Really black,'" she repeated. "Who've you been talking to, anyway?"

"Not the right people," I said, since I wasn't about to mention Lucius. "That's one of the reasons I'm glad I'm here."

She lowered her chin and caught my eye. "Why else?"

"Well, I didn't know people put cream cheese in sushi, but that was delicious."

"Boys are always hungry," she said.

"So, you can talk about punks and boys, but there's no such thing as really black?"

"Nope." She shook her head. "You're black, too. You're stuck with us."

Us.

The word made me grin. My grin made her grin. Her grin made me laugh and she joined in. The laughter paused and we looked at each other. I tried to think of a smooth way to lean over the arm of the couch and kiss her. Then there was a key in the door. Bree walked in wearing a shoulder bag with some fringe on it and stared at me like a teacher who knows you're cutting up but can't prove it. Bree was the only white person in the room.

"How was work?" I asked.

Bree sighed. "Slow."

She works at the college bookstore. I have no clue what they do when it isn't the beginning of the semester.

"Tonight I found out that our couch looks like a tongue," Mona told her.

Bree glared at the couch.

"I'm sorry to hear about your grandma," I said.

"It's OK," she said. "Thanks."

Mona said, "We made sushi. And there's beer in the fridge."

Bree shook her head ever so slightly. "Think I'm just gonna go to my room."

We were quiet as she trudged off through the kitchen, then Mona said, "I need to go to bed soon. Opening shift tomorrow."

"Oof. Back to back?"

Mona stood up and stretched in a way that thrust her chest at me. "Yeah. I'll walk you to the door." The door was fifteen feet away, tops. I appreciated the sentiment, though. I needed a second to find my legs.

Mona stood in the middle of the room, the hanging light fixture glinting above her head like a fairyland halo. I stood, wanting to stay with Mona and be "us," but not just the two of us. All of us. The crew of mixed kids and offbeat black kids I'd been seeking for years.

She asked, "You OK getting back?"

"Yeah, I'm fine," I said, rocking foot-to-foot. "You get your rest."

She said, "Thanks," and held my eye long enough for a jolt to flash from my shoulders and down my fingers, then she turned her head down a bit, so a single lock swung in front of her eye. I stepped to the middle of the room like I was about to do a fancy waltz, reached out, sucked my stomach in, and hugged her. She squeezed just above my love handles and I flexed a little as her breasts squished between my chest and stomach. After the squeeze, she pulled back. I loosened my arms and caught her upper back in my palm. When she looked to me, I leaned in to kiss her, shutting my eyes with six inches to go, opening them when hair that smelled like coconuts and weed blotted my lips. I sighed through my nose.

"Not now," Mona murmured into my shoulder, the puff of her breath dampening my shirt.

She stepped out of arm's reach and smiled.

It was early and I knew there was a basement show nearby, where a couple dozen dudes were probably jostling each other and spilling beer. I started biking home, wanting to pretend that hanging out with Mona was my regular life. It's not just that I needed more than white guys in my life, I also needed more than just guys.

The thick air slid across my temples and the trees rustled in slow motion. I gasped at how my heart felt like a metal bucket, the top tipping a wave of silver water, and how this hope in Mona did nothing more than show how few prospects I had.

How soon if not now? Would it be the next time I saw her? It was balmy, love weather, bare-skin-turned-gold-from-the-streetlamp weather, sex-under-open-windows weather, and I hated being alone.

**SEVEN** At the corner of Allen, the side street with the muddy median, Lucius hopped out of the shadows and onto my handlebars, wearing a black, white, and yellow Pittsburgh Penguins jersey. The hockey sweater's synthetic fabric slid across my chin as I leaned forward to pedal. The top-heavy bike wove left under the Robert E. Lee statue on Monument Avenue, Lee's horse's balls dangling high above our heads, the ass pointing north at the black neighborhoods just across Broad Street.

Racism here is often fancier than the Dixie flag bumper stickers you see next to race car logos on pickup trucks. Lee is one of four statues of famous Confederates on Monument Avenue. It's the ritziest street in the Fan, with a wide, grassy median, beautiful old town houses, and a new monument to a famous slaver every few blocks.

"Think I played that well?"

Lucius snorted and said, "She definitely knows how you feel."

We bumped over cobblestones and into the dark street on the other side of the avenue.

"I just kinda got gabbing and couldn't stop," I said. "So, what next? You think I've still got a chance?"

"Pssh, who knows, man." The back of his durag fluttered in my face. "If she wants it to happen, you'll end up alone together. Worst case, you got someone to talk to . . . and you keep talking."

"That's a good worst case," I said.

"Mmm-hmm."

"That's building a black community!" I pedaled hard.

"I guess," he said.

"That's the type of thing that might get a man his Black Card."

Lucius sighed and his breath smelled like a peach blunt wrap. "Keep building, bruh."

I took a right toward the beginning of wide, quiet Stuart Avenue. Thanks to the weed and beer, the neighborhood was less a place than a slideshow, with a new image blinking into focus every few seconds: cars parked under a tree with someone's porch light turning the leaves to silhouettes, the gray pavement stretching from a manhole to some headlights at the end of the block, a wrought-iron porch with white wicker furniture.

A beat-up sedan with a light-up pizza delivery sign on the roof nosed out of an alley and we swerved. Lucius shouted then reached back and slapped my shoulder a few times. "Keep with it, man. Don't be crashin' us."

"Dawg, watch it." I let one hand loose to push his away.

"Dawg," he imitated in a nasal voice.

"Hey," I said when I caught my breath. "Mona doesn't seem

too hung up on having her Black Card or being black enough or whatever."

"That's why your corny ass likes her."

"I guess so," I said.

"And that's probably why you started running your jibs and called her white-acting," he said. "You thought she could relate."

I pedaled harder and we bombed through a four-way stop by the grammar school, veering left onto Strawberry Street.

A siren whooped so loud that I swerved again, then coasted over to a nearby hydrant to let the fire truck or ambulance or whatever pass. The bike stopped, but Lucius didn't. He landed leaning forward, the back of his durag flapping like a superhero cape as he disappeared into the dark playground, sneaker slaps echoing off the brick school. By the time I figured out what was up, it was too late for me to run, too.

A cop car cut right and hemmed me in, red and blues splashing the street around me. The passenger window came down and a white man said, "Get your ID out."

Us. Had Mona and the slang I'd been trying a minute before conjured this cop?

The police brutality scenes from every black '90s movie jumped into my mind, all pistol whips, nightsticks, and racial epithets. I straddled my bike and fumbled in my back pocket, thinking of the African guy the cops shot in New York because they thought his wallet was a weapon.

The cop marched around the front of the car, short and stern, with a jutting, 1950s movie star chin. He stopped next to the hydrant, and I felt guilty for hoping he read me as white.

Last time I benefited from looking white, I lost my Black Card. But Lucius would say, "You extra-light-skinned brothers always got something to prove. If five-oh thinks you're a white man, let them keep thinking it. Save yourself a whooping."

Even on the curb, the cop was shorter than my six feet. I met his eye then looked away, twice.

"Do you know why I pulled you over?" he asked.

"No." I shook my head and his eyes burned into me. "Probably not for speed—"

"Did you see that stop sign back there?"

"Oh, uh—"

"ID, please." He cupped an impatient palm.

He scraped my knuckles with my license and did the same dick-hurt walk back to his car. While he was in there, my stomach flipped and I burped seaweed, then ran my tongue down the roof of my mouth and tasted old weed smoke. Nothing on me, just in me. My parents always said to be careful because I could get searched whenever. Lucius agrees, and usually makes me carry the weed, with the instructions to "walk with a tight ass and fall back a few feet if we see five-oh."

The short cop hopped back onto the curb and returned on light feet. With a ceremonious flair, like God giving Moses the commandments, he ripped the top sheet off his notepad. His biceps bulged where his short sleeve ended.

"Here's a ticket for running the stop sign."

"On my bike?" I asked.

I was getting high-pitched and whiny. The ticket dangled between us, damp in the summer night.

"The same laws apply to all vehicles on the road," he rattled off.

There wasn't much to say to that, but I took a shot.

"Ah, come on."

"I already wrote it," he said. "It ain't goin' away. That's not how we do it."

I tried to snatch the ticket without looking, and missed. When I raised my eyes, the cop held it back and cocked his head.

"You been drinkin' tonight, sir?"

I didn't answer.

"Step away from the bicycle and follow me to the car," he commanded, taking a step back.

I put down the kickstand, sinking feeling growing as we marched around to the far side of the cruiser. I thought about how I needed to savor the moments where I felt smooth, because they never last.

Picture this diorama, from right to left: a red mountain bike on its kickstand in the middle of a side street; a cop car parked at a 45-degree angle with its lights flashing; a cop standing by the open driver's door, watching me blow into a breathalyzer that looks like a ray gun from an old sci-fi movie.

The cop's face lit up when the breathalyzer beeped, and he started hustling me toward his car, saying, "Better take you in to sleep it off. Can't have you on the road like this."

I said, "I could walk home from here," and he knocked the top of my head on the cruiser's door frame. When he got in the driver's seat, I asked, "What about my bike?"

"Forget the bike, Afro Puffs," he said, then shifted into reverse and sent my bike flying before gunning it to the corner and running a stop sign of his own.

I felt kidnapped, my city suddenly strange. Old town houses with tall windows and peaked roofs flew by outside the windows of the stuffy car. When watching them gave me the spins, I looked around me for a seat belt that didn't exist.

I hadn't been called Afro Puffs since high school. A few years and dozens of haircuts later and it still didn't feel good. I stared into the rearview at the cop's shadowy face, craning my head around to take in his sweat-clammy jawline, his short sideburns, his washed-out eyes. I subtracted a few years from his reflection, added short, Eminem-style bangs to his crewcut and saw my first wigger driving the police car.

"John Donahue!"

My swampy beer breath bounced back off the bulletproof glass and I wrinkled my nose. His eyes met mine in the mirror, then returned to the road, just slow enough that I'd know he was ignoring me. It was a gamble. He might treat me even worse to make up for lost time. I figured it was worth the risk and leaned up to the glass again. "You gonna let me go for high school's sake? I know you didn't like it there either."

Somehow, my breath didn't melt the glass. Donahue frowned this time. I flopped back in the seat and slipped out my phone.

To: Mason
At: 10:31 pm
Lomg story. Going 2 drunk tank. Gft mybike from Strawberry by schol? Dont call In a cop car

We took a right by the gas station where the skater guy from high school got robbed at gunpoint. A daddy-longlegs-looking homeless guy in front of the mini-mart stared, holding a white plastic bag like a wizard's crystal ball. He turned blurry as Donahue hit the siren and floored it through the red light. There's nothing lonelier than waiting for a text in the back of a cop car.

 **EIGHT** Whoever designed the precinct had designed my high school, too. White spots of fluorescent light reflected off the polished brick walls. It smelled like a dusty basement. Donahue placed a palm on my back, inches above my cuffed-together wrists, and hustled me in so fast my toes skipped across the scuffed linoleum floor.

He shouted, "Got another one here!" at a heavyset guy behind the front desk, who looked up reluctantly, eyes slow as mud.

I was fifteen again, before I met Lucius, hoping to discover a group of like-minded skaters every time I turned a corner at my new school, constantly let down. Where was Lucius?

I couldn't lift my feet fast enough to keep up with Donahue, and I stumbled toward a wall of cell bars. He grabbed the cuffs and pain shot through my shoulders until I stood facing a jail cell where half a dozen men glided like sharks in an aquarium. My toes clenched while I fought the urge to bolt in any direction. I'd never been somewhere and not been allowed to leave.

My arms swung free and Donahue pushed me into the cell,

then I heard the bars clang shut, just like on my gangsta rap tapes. I stood on the concrete floor, taking a couple quavering breaths as I slipped into a fish-eyed stare that passed over hard-heads and teachers, too vacant to be a challenge but too steely to seem spaced out. I thought I'd left that stare in high school.

I looked up. The only white guy was middle-aged with a walrus mustache and a curtain of stringy brown hair hanging around his bald spot. He pointed at me from the bottom bunk along the right wall, saying, "See, the odds are starting to change."

No matter how many times my father warned me about having to act better than the white boys because I stand out, white people tend to think I'm white. If Lucius was here I'd have to say something, but this felt like a "choose your battles" scenario, and I figured I'd hear worse before I left. I stood by the cell door. A guy who I think was around thirty turned from the toilet, zipping his jeans then hitching their loose waistband and slurring, "Go on, mang. He ain't know you."

The white guy smiled and looked at me for confirmation. I maintained the stare, eyes dry, swaying if I looked at one thing for too long. The weed from Mona's place still poked at the corners of my brain. I'd never wanted to be high less than I did right then.

The guy who'd been pissing looked to me, too, and said, "Tha'sha bwoah?"

"Huh?"

Lucius subtracts points every time I can't understand a blaccent. The white guy was still smiling in the corner of my eye. The black guy spoke louder: "THA'SHA BWOAH?"

I still didn't catch what he was saying. A slim brother with a peanut head pushed off the back wall and eased forward, pointing at the white guy and saying, "Nigga, he ax if you know this man here."

"Oh." I clicked my tongue on the roof of my mouth. "No."

Whatever mojo Mona had given me was gone. Slim and Loose-Pants folded into exaggerated laughs. We weren't gonna buddy up against the white guy. Even through my haze, I felt self-conscious, wondering if Slim called me "nigga" because he could tell I was black, or because he called everyone that.

I didn't just need Lucius to watch. I needed him to guide me.

The white guy leaned back in the bottom bunk. There was a homeless guy in a dusty gray suit coat lying down, facing the wall, on the bunk above him. He shuffled his feet, in gym socks that might have been white in the '90s, then stretched his bottom leg, spread his toes, and farted a long outboard-motor blast.

Loose-Pants and Slim yelled "Oh!" and covered their faces. Another guy looked up from the far side of the white guy's bunk. He'd had his head in his hands, and I saw he was a little younger than me, with frizzy cornrows. He still looked half asleep, the rest disgusted and amused. The white guy's eyes drooped shut, the creepy Zen smile still on his face. The place already smelled like mold, bleach, and old beer, and the fart didn't change that at all.

Slim asked me, "Why *you* here?"

"Drunk biking, I guess."

Loose-Pants asked, "You got one a them Ducati?"

"Huh?"

Slim said, "This again? With your Daisy Dukes ass."

My cut-off Dickies felt silly. A tough situation calls for tougher clothing. Maybe some armor or a hazmat suit or at least some long, baggy shorts like Lucius wears.

I looked at Slim long enough for him to say, "What?" then Loose-Pants repeated himself, "One of them Ducati. What kinda motorcycle you got?"

"Oh. No," I said. "It's a mountain bike. Like a bicycle."

I held imaginary handlebars and wobbled my knees, pedaling.

"He said 'bicycle'!" Slim laughed.

The kid on the bunk smiled too, taking in the new low man on the totem pole, then said, "This nigga look like Justin Timberlake."

Loose-Pants turned away, disappointed.

The kid said, "Timberlake ass," and everyone ignored him.

Slim asked, "How you gonna get locked up for," he made his voice a little deeper and enunciated, "drunk biking?"

Loose-Pants guffawed.

I said, "Good question."

"You live in Henrico or something?"

"Nah, the West End. By the 'woods."

There are two West Ends in Richmond: the white one, which starts near the suburban Henrico County line, and the black one, which starts closer to Downtown and has a bunch of avenues that end with 'wood: Idlewood, Rosewood, Parkwood . . .

Richmond's a small city and I actually live two blocks from the 'woods, in the yuppified Museum District. I'd claimed the 'woods to sound blacker.

Slim asked, "You know this bright nigga Shamel, live down off Harrison?"

"Nah."

I had to piss, but didn't want to walk farther into the cell, turn my back, or start a conversation about how my junk measured up. I'd been so close to home. I would have been asleep right then, but instead I was trapped in jail. It wasn't fair and I was scared I was gonna cry. Who'd get hurt from some drunk biking?

The cops pushed a bulky, country-looking white boy with wire-rimmed glasses and a buzz cut into the cell, and he paced, muttering and radiating a mix of anger and sport deodorant. I leaned on the empty wall and stared at the floor, hearing the new guy grumble the words "dear," "lord," and "bitch" a good few times. We didn't do anger well at my house growing up, going from catlike soothing to full-on yelling, missing the ticked-off middle ground that I heard so much from the hood.

Getting thrown in jail was a black stereotype that my parents had feared I'd make good on. But being in jail threw it all into contrast. I didn't belong there. But did any of the other guys with me feel like they belonged in jail? I snuck a glance around the cell. Doubt it.

How would Lucius handle this situation? He'd probably post up on a bottom bunk, legs spread, elbows on knees, laughing knowingly at jokes I hardly picked up on.

Things went on without me, and I figured on staying invisible, leaning against the concrete wall like I might melt into it and come out free on the other side.

Eventually, I slid down and tried to stare at an empty section of the opposite wall. I couldn't focus, and it made my eyes hurt. After a few long blinks, I shut them to the bright lights, figuring that if trouble was coming my way I wouldn't be able to do much even if I could see it.

I hovered in a half-sleep while the guys around me kept up a steady hum of trash talk. With my eyes closed, I could imagine us all waiting for a bus, or on break from a crappy job.

Then my phone rang.

I whipped it out of my pocket so fast, it sent my bright, woven Guatemalan wallet spinning out toward the middle of the cell, right by the country-looking white guy's feet. I dove after the wallet, clapping the phone to my ear in time to hear Mason go, "What the hell, dude?"

On one knee, I threw my hand at the wallet and cupped Country's puffy white sneaker, which had just landed on it.

"Oh, he got a phone, too!" Country shouted, reaching down and trying to grab it from my ear.

"Get off!" I shouted into the phone. "Mason, I'm in—"

Country pulled me toward him and I toppled sideways, out of what had probably been a yoga pose.

"How he gonna have a phone up in here?" someone else shouted.

"Lemme call my sister," another guy yelled.

One guy said, "Hey, quiet. Grab his feet," in a raspy stage whisper, then I heard footsteps rushing toward me from behind.

Mason was sounding alarmed as hell in the phone, which was muffled by my cheek. Hands flipped me onto my back, and I started kicking, while three or four guys grunted and grabbed at me, trying to pull the phone away, lifting the wallet off the floor, and snaking hands into my pockets as I rolled back and forth.

Then the cell door roared open. There were three amazingly loud metallic bangs and a bassy cop voice shouted, "Hey! Break it up, unless you want a piece of this taser."

Everyone took two steps back from me, and I got up on my elbows and saw a bald-headed black cop standing in the door to the cell, holding a nightstick to the still reverberating bars, with a taser gun in his other hand. An even taller blond cop stood behind him, hand on holster.

"You." The bald-headed cop pointed his taser at me. "Stand up."

Little electrical plug-looking things dangled from the taser gun's barrel.

Before I could obey, Mason shouted "Hello?" into the phone and his distorted electronic voice buzzed throughout the cell.

Baldhead looked confused, then saw the phone, still clutched in my hand, and said, "Where'd you get this contraband? Get up and get out here now."

We stood in an interrogation room. The blond cop looked bored, but Baldhead was livid. He'd snatched my phone, and now it bulged in his pants pocket.

"Name," he demanded.

I told him, and he left to check the records while the blond cop and I didn't quite look at each other after he told me to "take a seat" and I obeyed, pulling a plastic chair out from under a fake wood table.

Baldhead busted back in. "Why are you here?"

"John Donahue brought me in."

He glared.

"Officer John Donahue," I added.

"How did you get this phone in here?" he asked.

"I didn't get searched," I said. "I just got put in the cell. I had a wallet, too, but the guys in the cell took it from me."

The blond cop started to look agitated, and looked toward the door while Baldhead stared me down.

"For real," I said.

They told me to stay put and shut the door behind themselves as they walked out of the bare little room. After a few minutes, I rested my head on the smooth tabletop.

With no clock, I couldn't tell just how slowly the night was crawling by. The room was hot and stale and sometimes I thought the air was too thick to breathe and I'd drown. Sometime after my eyes turned to cotton balls, my throat a strip of carpet, the blond cop came in, plunked my phone and open wallet on the table in front of me, and led me out onto Meadow Street, which I've heard white boys call "Ghetto Street." I didn't look back.

Just leaving was beautiful. The humid night gleamed in the last moments before dawn. The air was a shower stall. As I slid my cash- and Black Card–free wallet into my pocket, I realized that Donahue never actually gave me the ticket for running the stop sign. That made me smile. I took a deep, wet breath, and started walking away fast like I could leave that mess behind.

Something wasn't right in there, but I wasn't going back to figure out what.

I felt like a burden when I texted Mason.

Out now thank you sorry

 **NINE** I was a mile from home, head clanging for coffee from the gas station, but scared it'd give me the bubble guts. I trudged to Floyd Avenue, rising sun warming me from the right.

The streets felt fresh and promising, contrasting my insides where something horrible festered, radiating out, so people might see and know I'd spent the night in jail. I wiggled my fingers and looked at my hands. I needed to understand what had happened before I told anyone.

I walked on, practically smelling coffee and newspapers in the Fan's early morning kitchens, craving the comforts I'd dismissed upon getting into punk: peace and quiet, a good night's sleep, vegetables, a live-in girlfriend, and a car to make my world bigger than biking distance.

A cyclist blew by from behind me and shouted, "'Sup!" in a nasal voice.

I jumped. It was Russell's roommate, Clay, the type of gossip who likes nothing more than thinking he knows something you don't. I put grubby finger to grubby forehead and gave a weak salute, praying he wouldn't stop. He kept pedaling, likely toward his job at the health food store.

Ooh, my bike.

I looped up Strawberry Street with a sinking panic, stretching my stride as if the minute I'd save was the one that'd keep my bike. I saw the red hydrant. I saw a silver SUV parked just beyond the hydrant. I saw the empty patch of pavement where my bike had been. I stood in the street and rotated by the SUV. A good Samaritan had not leaned my bike against the school fence, tucked it by some trash cans in the alley, set it on a nearby porch, or played a prank and dangled it from the phone line.

My bike was gone.

It cost a week's pay.

It took me everywhere.

I'd left my skateboard who-knows-where a few months ago. I was more stuck than ever.

If you can afford a car, you'll drive that. So, if you ride a bike, you need a bike. And if you steal bikes, you're scum.

Sun glowed on the bricks of the school's east wall then glistened as a sharp pain filled my throat. Damn. I was crying on the street by a grade school. I wanted to say, "These things don't happen," but look at the last few days. The Black Card. The drunk tank. The bike. They do.

I walked fast back toward Floyd Avenue. At the corner, my lungs throbbed and I let out a long, shuddering sigh, then propped a hand on the edge of the school's black fence and blew a snot rocket onto its base. A middle-aged woman in office clothes and ratty jogging shoes looked up from pacing her dog back and forth on a nearby patch of grass. I kept moving, head hot and swimmy.

I had two options: fall into bed and get woken up by the sun in an hour, or get some espresso and keep rolling. Mona was at the coffee-shop and I was rawer than I'd ever been. Why not let her see that and know me?

I'd play it a little cool. I'd keep my distance so she couldn't smell me. Can you get morning breath if you never really fell asleep?

**TEN** The coffeehouse was on a corner in Carytown, a quaint and quirky shopping district with buckling brick sidewalks. There's a record store, used book store, and second-run movie theater sprinkled in between boutiques with vowel-heavy names like Lulabella, that are meant for fancy southern white ladies to say. It's the neighborhood that you show out-of-towners so they don't think the whole city is a dump.

In true Richmond style, Carytown is a one-way street. It runs east from Windsor Farms, a rich neighborhood with fake gas lamps instead of streetlights, where you'd better have a plunger or an apron if you're not white. Then it ends just south of the Fan, in the hood by the precinct and bus depot. Also in true Richmond style, this change from old money to no money happens in just over a mile.

My job sat smack in the middle. It was a dusty coffee shop with funky woodwork throughout, dim lighting, and coffee grounds embedded in the linoleum floor. You could get a big cup of strong coffee or some fancy double-mocha-half-caf-skim creation there. It was just right.

Aside from free espresso, I wanted a dramatic scene to play out with Mona when I walked in. Maybe she'd abandon the line and bust out from behind the counter to hug me. Maybe she'd realize something was wrong and tease out the news that I'd been oppressed by the pigs. I'd even settle for a knowing look, held just long enough as she stirred a mocha. Or a quick hello on some "We're so close that I don't even have to act polite" type stuff. Anything to prove that we'd only hit pause after the night before.

Instead, I found Russell dead on his feet at the register, a comet trail of dried drool on his cheek, pop punk whining quietly on the house stereo.

I waited by the milk bar while Russell rang out one of the blondes from the hair salon down the block, wondering where Mona was and if Mason had already blown up my spot about the drunk tank.

The hairdresser opened her can of diet soda then sang out a goodbye. Russell gave her a dazed smile then beckoned me over. "Hey, uhh."

His stubble was beginning to soften.

"Thought you were off today," I said.

Part of my plan was seeing if he wanted to meet up for breakfast, so I could tell someone about last night, then maybe move toward a nap before our show.

"I got called in," he said, with a sense of purpose. "Mona's in the hospital."

"What?" I said. "What happened?"

Did she get sick from the sushi?

He sighed. "I guess, she was in bed and a burglar attacked her." He caught my eye. "Like, tried to rape her. But didn't. But they like got in a fight and he stabbed her."

"Come on, dude," I said. "That's not funny."

I was almost impressed that he'd think of a joke that messed up, and started looking through the open doorway to the kitchen, expecting Mona to walk out and wave.

"Come on, yourself," he said. "That's why I'm here." He wiped his hands down his apron until gravity took over and they fell to his sides.

When he said "come on, yourself" and didn't laugh at the innuendo, I knew he wasn't playing. I gripped the edge of the counter and asked, "She's gonna be OK?"

"Yeah." Russell nodded, then looked over my shoulder. While he pumped a coffee for the tired-eyed suit from the real estate office next door, I tried to understand how something so random and terrible could happen, and trees wouldn't turn oily black, cars wouldn't explode, the world wouldn't stop.

I stepped aside again as the suit turned toward the milk bar. Russell said, "She called in from the hospital at like four."

Mona is the type of person who'd call in from the hospital. That's not the type of person who you picture something like this happening to.

"Shit."

What else can you say to that? I tried it again a little louder, "Shit," wishing I could go right into a loud, dramatic reaction. I just felt confused.

Russell and I looked away from each other for a second. The door closed behind the real estate guy.

"You're up early," Russell said. "Or still up?" He watched me, waiting for the rundown of last night.

"Early," I lied. "Couldn't sleep."

"Wish they'd called you in," he said, and my fear flashed, *Don't let him try and guilt me into taking over his shift.*

"Maybe next time," I said.

The prep fridge's metallic hum switched on while Russell screwed up his face and said, "Hopefully there isn't a next time, dude. Come on."

"You're right," I said. "Sorry. I'm so damn tired. So—"

"You were over there last night," he said, still watching me.

"Yeah, but I cut out around ten," I said. "I sure didn't see anything."

Had the burglar been watching and seen me leave? Would I have helped if I'd stayed over? Somewhere, Lucius was going, "See, you let all that out about feeling like a white boy and that kept you from being there to save the girl." Where the hell was Lucius, anyway?

"Mind if I grab a drink?" I asked.

Russell shook his head and waved the back of his hand at the kingdom behind him.

I pulled an espresso into the biggest to-go cup, then topped it off with dark roast. Mona had touched that espresso machine. Mona had touched that coffee pot. Mona had stacked those brown paper cups on the counter last night. Someone had tried to rape Mona.

"Ready for the show tonight?" Russell asked.

I thought, *No*, then said, "Jackson Ward, right? With those idiots from North Carolina?"

Russell looked at me sideways. "With Dog Day Afternoon. They're from Gainesville."

"Ahh."

"Were you talking about Kill All Their Infernal Soldiers?" he asked. "They the idiots?"

"Yeah." I nodded, did a half-smile. "Who else?"

"Well, they're coming here in a week or so," Russell said. "Tonight's different. But maybe we can sing some karaoke after."

I laughed, dislodging some phlegm. "My amp's still in the van."

I felt as stunned as Russell looked, and lurched like a sleep-deprived mummy, getting a wet nose from sipping coffee backwards. I wanted to do something. There was nothing I could do. I lifted my coffee in a grim cheers to Laptop then dragged myself home, the new sun strange and sinister.

ONE TIME

ONE

Caring is exhausting. My friends and I don't do it well. That's why we chug beer, scream songs, and make sarcastic comments. But then the universe flexes and someone overdoses, or a family member dies, or a burglar stabs your coworker, and you just can't laugh it off.

So, punks, this is your emergency plan for when you get out of the drunk tank and your crush is in the hospital:

Sip the coffee. You're not gonna nap, and it's hot enough to flower in your throat, but not so hot that it burns. Drink deeper.

Feel the need to do something. But what? Fight a cop? Walk the streets looking for someone who is carrying a knife and a photo of Mona?

Punch the side of the couch. Hit the frame by accident. Feel drained when the knuckle pain subsides. Stiffen when you once again feel the need to perform your caring.

Text her: *Im sorry to hear about what happened. I hope youre Ok*

Realize you should have called instead but worry that following up so fast would be overkill.

Think about how calling will not heal her or erase the drunk tank's grime. Picture a shadow creeping through her apartment.

Wonder why you're not weeping. Wonder why, aside from a crumpled face and a few tears down the cheek, you haven't really let loose with the crying since that one time in high school when nothing in your new city felt satisfying or reliable. Wonder why there's a stack of bad things tottering on top of your heart, but they just won't fall.

There's golden brown knee hair. Below it, faded navy corduroy love seat. Beyond that, flowery couch. Between couch and window, a bike-size space. Drifts of fine, dry dirt are sprinkled on the space's shining wood floor.

The cops owe you a bike and today's extra half hour of walking.

Call the cops on the cops.

It's weird to hear 911 ringing. You'd expect them to answer immediately. Picture a 911 operator gingerly setting down an iron then hustling to the phone.

"Yes, I'd like to report a stolen bicycle . . . Yes, I will hold."

There's enough time to start wondering about the point of this, but not enough time to act on that newfound doubt.

"I do. On Strawberry Street around ten fifteen, ten thirty last night. Officer John Donahue made me leave it unlocked while he detained me."

You are an outraged citizen, and this outrage will not stand.

The cop pauses, sighs, takes down info.

There's still a shadow in Mona's apartment.

TWO After my 911 call, I threw on Dad's old Curtis Mayfield LP, double checked to make sure the front door curtain was closed, then pushed a couple old bills and a fanzine aside on the coffee table and got ready to break up some weed on the back of one of Mason's stoner rock CDs. Funny how most of my friends listen to grating punk rock when they're high and Mason doesn't even smoke and subsists on a steady diet of groovy riffs. You'd think the music would mellow him out.

When I opened the plastic bag of weed, bass began rumbling up the block from some car's boomin' system. It set off a car alarm near the corner, the wailing alarm melding with the hip-hop snare cracks, creating a chaotic beat that drowned out Curtis Mayfield as the car drew closer.

As the stink of weed wafted up from the bag, the rap beat plateaued, my curtains fluttered, and a wave of coffee cruised across the top of the paper cup. Then the bass stopped, then the car alarm, and my stereo played twenty seconds of the busy congas and wistful organ of "Little Child Running Wild" before Lucius slid through the front door in grape-colored sunglasses and matching velour tracksuit. "Aye, you smokin'?"

"Figured this'd bring you in."

"Figured right." He looked sideways at the bowl. He preferred blunts. Said I'd learn to roll one day.

I lit up. Curtis Mayfield's horns swelled into a series of dramatic punches.

"So, the drunk tank sucked," I said.

"Oh, word?" Lucius asked.

"Where were you?"

The stabs of strings started again on the record.

"Hey." He showed me palms. "What kinda brotha wants his friend to get locked up?"

"What kinda friend runs off on his friend in a bind?" I took a hit and held it in, giving him the icy eye until mine watered.

"I woulda been no help with the police."

"You were no help, anyway." I exhaled and coughed. "I needed you in my ear."

"I was there," he said.

I flipped him the bird.

"You survived, ain't you?" he asked.

For a moment, I remembered the hands of the guys in the drunk tank swarming over me. As I passed Lucius the bowl, a key scraped into the front door.

"Stick around," I murmured to Lucius. "This ain't all we got to talk about."

Mason appeared in the living room, waving a hand in front of his face to clear away the little bit of smoke. He lost the typical "dad about to lose his patience" tension in his cheeks, drooped his eyelids Hookah Guy–style and said, "This early, brah?"

"Or this late, man," I said. "I'm still up."

Mason sat on the edge of the couch, cast a wary eye at the bowl, and asked, "What happened last night?"

I sighed. "Well," I said. "You didn't get my bike, for starters."

"I tried!" He jumped up, protesting a little too much. "By the time I got over there, it was gone!"

"Hmm."

For some reason, I just didn't believe him. Lucius agreed, judging by his pursed lips.

"I tried," Mason repeated. "Felt kinda stupid walking around there, searching for nothing."

"OK," I said, thinking, *I'll tell you what feels stupid.* "Well, thanks anyway."

"So, you gonna tell me what happened?" he asked. "It's not every day I get a text message from a police car. And what was going on when I called?"

The hot guitar on "Freddie's Dead" kicked in. I paused and nodded, then said, "Basically, I ran a stop sign on my bike, and got pulled over."

"Weird."

"Right?" I said. "There was no one around—"

"Except the cop," Mason interrupted.

"Right. Still, you'd think they'd have better things to do," I said, thinking, *Like protect Mona.*

"Aye, ask a cop," Lucius broke in. "Ain't nothin' better to them than messin' with a brotha."

"Yeah," said Mason. "And they arrested you?"

"Yeah," I said. "Made me take a breathalyzer. And I was a little drunk."

He sighed. So did I. Lucius slid the bowl across the coffee table and I twirled it in a circle with my finger.

"That sucks," Mason said. "But it's a little gangsta too, right?"

Curtis Mayfield sang, "Hey heyyy" in his perfect falsetto. I said, "I guess. I mean, I *was* doin' Black Stuff."

Mason laughed. "Yup."

Lucius gave me a look like "Really?" for talking outside the family.

"So, when you called," I said, "I was in the . . . drunk tank, and it started a fight or something because the other guys there were trying to take my phone."

"It's weird that the cops didn't take your phone away before they put you in there."

"Right?" I said. "They didn't give me a ticket, either. Maybe police stations are different than on TV."

"Guess so," Mason said, and stood up. "Don't forget, show tonight at seven."

"Right, right," I said, and squinted at a new beam of sun coming through the window.

He slipped back into his Hookah Guy impression and croaked, "You gonna be ready to rock?"

"You know it, brah," I said in my own hippy-dippy voice, plucking air bass with my pointer and middle finger.

He walked into his room, bending his wrist back to ease the carpal tunnel pain from practicing guitar.

Lucius headed into the kitchen and I lay back down. I hadn't forgotten about Mona. Not at all. But I couldn't find a way to work her into the conversation with Mason.

The record ended, and I started drifting off to the patter of Mason's shower. Next I knew, Mason had his usual backpack on over his work polo, and was easing the door open with his guitar case between him and the wall, dangling from his left hand. I shut my eyes and didn't open them again until the sun was buttery, the coffee cool on the floor by my phone. I remembered nothing for a moment, then saw Mona, Loose-Pants, and Slim between my face and the shadowy ceiling as I blinked.

THREE I avoided explaining my missing bike by telling Russell to meet me at the show. Lucius and I had made the half-hour walk together, talking about Mona, me shouting "Right?" when he said, "How they gonna be there to lock you up for running a got-damn stop sign on your bike, but they can't keep someone from breaking into her apartment?"

After that, I shook my head going "Damn" for a whole block, then Lucius and I cleared our minds by practicing our "muhfukkas" until we hit campus.

As we passed the library, I rubbernecked, wanting to see Hookah Guy and feel in on the joke, bringing back some of the punk rock cockiness that made my friends and me laugh at try-hards who moved into the dorms and went all out with a new identity, going mega goth in baggy black pants, wearing layers of fraternity gear, or lugging a hookah around campus. Trying too hard is never good. But punks do it, too, and I've made my share of jokes about Brand New Painted Leather Jacket Guy, Weird Glasses Guy, Won't Stop Talking About a New Genre of Music That Sounds Crappy Guy, Gonna DJ Now Guy, "I'm

Mainly into Jazz Now" Guy, Actually Cares About His Job Guy, and Put "Free Beer" on the Flyer and Undercover Cops Showed Up Guy.

 **FOUR**

The sun lowered and the evening stayed sticky. Russell and I stood under a tree in a Jackson Ward backyard, thickening half-chugged sodas with pours from a bottle of cheap bourbon. Lucius had split off at the chain-link gate, saying, "I ain't going in there so your nasty lil' friends can bump into me."

The punks arrived, white, at least two boys per girl, clutching twelve-packs and forties of beer and walking up the alley in small groups, or clamping lit smokes in their lips while they locked bikes to the fence along the side street.

Summertime Richmond's a special thing. The steaming streets are empty of most college kids. The skeleton crew of friends who stick around pick a porch to drink on, talk about biking to the river more than they actually bike to the river, home in on a house full of girls who had just been freshmen, get buzzed with random hippies from work, and see the bands who come through on their own summer breaks. I'd been missing that, even if I knew I was getting too old for it.

I needed some of that comfort and wonder, but found myself staring at each kid, my usual excitement over another audience member erased by questions: Has this kid ever been stabbed? Raped? Said "nigger"? Had to move in with their grandparents?

———

Russell's roommate, Clay, skulked up with a twelve-pack under one arm, free hand flapping the front of his loose black T-shirt for breeze.

"Anyone play?" he asked.

"Nope," said Russell, sighing at the broken silence.

"Figures," whined Clay.

Clay had a shrill voice, hunched shoulders, a permanent sneer, and BO that smelled like the bulk bins at a health food store. He was the type of person who'd say it's typical that *you're* there when you run into him in the beer aisle at cut-off time. I didn't care for the guy, but I saw him all the time. That's Richmond.

Clay hid his beers behind a tree root, lit a smoke, and said, "I heard Dog Day Afternoon asked for a hundred-dollar guarantee." Paper Fire had averaged half that on tour, and that's typical.

"They've got some nerve, trying to get back to Florida," cracked Russell.

"It's not about that. It's not about money," Clay shouted, dousing his smoke as he opened a shook-up beer. He had more ideas than follow-through. I'd seen him a couple weeks before, taking his bass to jam with some guy and get "the spirit of jazz and the drive of old-school hardcore . . . but with a drum machine."

"What do you know about touring, Clay?" I asked.

"You'd be surprised," he scoffed.

"Hey, now," Russell cut him off. "We need to chill, especially after what happened to Mona."

"That's the girl from your job," Clay stated.

"Yeah, duh," I said.

"Chill," said Russell. "Here." He handed me the whiskey.

I sipped and blew the fumes out of my nose. It hit me that Russell was pretty shook up about Mona. The whole city seemed different. Like, inside each house or car could be a rapist, or one of their victims.

"You guys ever been broken in on?"

"Yeah, remember?" Russell said.

"Ohh." I nodded.

We sipped our drinks and looked around while Clay told the story, again, about how he'd come home from a morning shift to find the front door ajar, no one home, and everyone's VCRs and DVD players missing from their rooms.

"Some crackhead was probably a block away with a shopping cart full of our stuff." Clay pushed an imaginary handle. "Can't believe the cops didn't get him."

I was tired of the cops, and sometimes I think "crackhead" is another word for "nigger," but I laughed along with Russell and let Clay ease the whiskey from my hand. Everyone in the Fan has a break-in story, but our brushes with violence tend to stop there.

"Y'all ever been stabbed, though?" I asked, feeling bolder.

Russell said, "Nah, of course not."

"Anyone ever try to rape—" I said, and Clay cut me off, screeching something about, "One time during Dungeons and Dragons . . ."

Russell sensed my prickling annoyance and interrupted Clay, pointing at me and saying, "Ya know, he was the last one to see her. He had dinner at her place last night."

"Well, her roommate—" I said.

Clay went, "Dinner end at six in the morning?"

"Huh?" Russell asked, pausing midway into reaching for Clay's twelve-pack.

"That was you I saw on Floyd this morning, right?" Clay guffawed. "Sounds like dinner was pretty good."

"Dinner was great," I said, then looked at Russell. "But I left at ten."

"He lives off Floyd," Russell told Clay.

"Down by us?" Clay asked, and I wondered if he ever spent the night at a girl's, then figured he hadn't, because I would have heard all about it if he did.

"All right, look," I said, and snatched back the whiskey. "I spent the night in the drunk tank down on Meadow." Liquor immediately felt like the wrong thing to be holding.

Russell grimaced. "Whaaat?"

Clay perked up for the gossip. That's all it was to him. Clay and Russell had never been arrested. They expected me to spin a tale that started with "It was ridiculous, dude. I had *sixteen* beers . . ."

I shrugged. "I just . . . ran a stop sign on my bike and got pulled over and they gave me a breathalyzer. It suck—"

"Did you drop the soap?" asked Clay.

"Fuck you, man," I said with more force than planned, then looked over my shoulder at the house, hoping a band was starting.

"Saw-*ree*," muttered Clay, like I was the prick.

Everyone sipped on something or other. A gaggle of black-clad crusty punks chased a dirty dog around the back porch, and one of them drunkenly slammed into the railing and shouted, "Sod off, Mossy!" in a fake English accent while her friends laughed and the dog licked her grimy face.

There was a peal of distorted guitar from the inside, then the idle punch of a bass string as someone adjusted an amp. We shuffled on our feet and I saw the people beyond us flicking their smokes aside and trudging indoors.

"Let's go in, dudes," said Russell.

The first band were all twentyish with long hair, proud of their van, just back from that first short tour down the coast, their music better than I wanted to admit.

They'd set up to play in a bedroom at the back of the first floor. I wedged behind the chest-high bass amp, nodded to the drummer, and the band roared to life without a hello to the crowd. Sweat flew as fuzzed-out guitars and thick snare hits ricocheted off the close walls. The handful of people crammed up front—transplants from a year or two ago who I never got to know—became an undulating blob of black T-shirts and silver beer cans. When I set my empty on the windowsill behind me, I saw a pile of faces watching through the glass and the hot room became a limbo. Each face was a blank that I couldn't fill in. I felt like I was chasing a train.

We knew the last song was the last song because it started with a dramatic build of bass and drums. The topless, teenage-skinny singer boy pogoed to the beat with a mic cord for a tail, and I jumped too, joining the crowd's "Go! Go! Go!" chant. The old house's sodden floor buckled with each leap until the guitar elbowed its way in and everyone landed, arms waving.

This was the release that I'd wanted, but in that realization,

I whisked myself back out of the moment and frowned at my hands, clapping stupidly in front of me.

Screaming the last verse, the singer appeared at my side, sea lion slick when he brushed my arm and threw open the window. The people on the back porch stepped back, raising beers in appreciation. The singer dove over the sill and onto the porch, kicking the bass amp. I clamped my hands onto the top to steady it. By the time I turned back, he was a flash of sweat-shiny back in the dusk, dragging the mic cord into the dark as displaced shouts exploded from the PA speaker to my left. The song ended with a crash of cymbals, the mic cord draped over the drum set like caution tape.

Through the applause, the room's heat shifted from electric to oppressive. I said, "Nice show," to the bassist. He smiled as I slipped out from behind the amp. The wall was wet to the touch. My head was a grinding gear, waiting to catch a cog.

I stepped onto the back deck, twenty degrees cooler but still hot. Multiply the front row by five. That's how many people were standing in the grass below me, blowing cheap smokes over warm beer, the dark yard a ballet of glowing red dots.

Beyond was Jackson Ward, a black neighborhood that was nicknamed the Harlem of the South during the Jazz Age. Its wide streets are lined with beautiful brick row houses and ornate wrought-iron porches, salvaged when the city burned at the end of the Civil War. My father was born blocks from the show, and whenever I went to the neighborhood, I'd look at the street corners and imagine him younger, standing there with a hokey old rhythm 'n' blues song in his head. But I'd always felt disconnected from the place. It didn't feel right that my only reason for being in a black neighborhood was to hang out with white people.

"You think they put it outside because it's too loud in there?" Russell was bent at the waist, whiskey bottle dangling from his right hand, peering into a hamster cage sitting on a plastic table along the railing to my left.

"I dunno, dude," I said, and commandeered the whiskey. When I tipped the bottle to my mouth, the porchlight gleamed off an air bubble rising through the brown booze.

Russell was trying to poke his finger between the wires on the side of the cage. A girl in dark jeans and a tank top raised a super-sculpted eyebrow at Russell's butt, then fixed her eyes on her friends in the yard. Walking down the steps, she dragged on her cigarette then blew out a haze of smoke as she passed Mason, Clay, and these nineteen-year-old dorm girls with matching bangs who Mason always talked to.

Somewhere in town, a dinner party was going on. Nothing fancy, but some interesting food with plenty of vegetables, a spice I'd never heard of, and an ingredient from the health food store. An evenly matched group of men and women—not all white—would be talking about books that aren't about bands, music that doesn't scream, and cultural stuff I wasn't even up on because I was busy getting drunk and breaking into a hamster cage.

"Where is it?" grunted Russell, still poking.

I leaned in, a swell of whiskey crashing into my brain. "Maybe in the little house!"

"Dude." Russell laughed. "He's got a little house!"

Paper Fire was playing last because we didn't want the show to get shut down before Dog Day Afternoon played. Deep down, below all the beer and the Mona and the drunk tank, something told me to slow down on the booze. But then I remembered the lurch as John Donahue floored it in the cop car, and the bottle angled up to my mouth again.

I swallowed, wiped my lips with the back of my hand, and shouted, "Where's our hamster buddy?" loud enough that people in the yard looked our way and Mason made a disapproving "Heyyy" sound before turning to the dorm girls with his nose up and his voice down.

The rest of the night comes back in flashes. Here are a few that connect the hamster break-in to 5 a.m., when I woke up puking in bed, throbs rising through my skull like radio signals:

Me on the deck giving all the white people in the yard below a fisheye stare, imagining them doing top-secret white stuff, like spinning a globe with lacrosse sticks.

Russell asking, "You OK to play?"

Me doing some innovative shadowbox-to-twirl move that ended with a stagger-jog to the center of the yard.

Clay helping Mason carry my amp into the house.

Mason warming up with some slow, heavy stoner-rock riff. Russell joining in on the drums. The look they share when I try to play along.

• • •

Me playing bass, alone, like you could zoom out with a camera on a helicopter until you saw me as an ant, alone in the desert with my amp.

I raise the pick, ready for the F-sharp I'm about to hit to shift the tectonic plates. For the following G to summon light-skinned Marcus Garvey's chariot from under the earth's crust. For the C to earn me a ride to Halfrica.

There is a rumble. Worried that the pick will be struck by lightning, I send it howling down at the awaiting string.

Lightning crackles from my amp as my bass string breaks and hangs loose, part unraveled, not even cleanly snapped.

A roof grows over the desert. Two dozen people appear along with the taste of stale beer and sweet whiskey, the smell of floor dust and cigarette butts, the wash of cymbals without bass to connect them to the buzzing guitar, all aimed right at my gut full of alcohol. I go to hit the third fret. My pick pulls the broken string free from the bass.

Mason's mouth is open, his chest puffed, his eyes bugged as he prepares to bellow the next line into the mic. He sees my broken string, and sings anyway. We can fix equipment mid-song. The most important part of a gig is not killing the momentum.

But I turn around and trip on my own guitar cord, then tumble into my amp. My face scratches across the speaker cover and onto the gritty floor, the amp topples backwards and props at an angle against the wall, where I'd been standing during the first band. The guitar and drums sputter out.

The room is pitching back and forth. The back of my tongue is tingling. I consider hopping out the window but turn, barrel through the crowd, and stumble out onto the deck, puking. My elbow skids across barf-slick wood. A handful of black-haired, highwater-wearing emo kids scatter.

My elbows are on the deck railing like it's the side of a pool.

Russell is patting my back as I puke into the yard. He says, "Let it all out, buddy."

It's the most tender thing someone has done for me in a while. Real tears mix with the wetness of throwing up as I retch one last time and sigh before pushing off the railing.

As I search for balance, my sneaker hooks in a plastic table leg, upending it, catapulting the hamster cage toward the back door.

I fall as blond cedar shavings scatter across the deck. Some stick in my puke, others sift between the boards, then the cute little hamster house rolls out, followed by an oblong bundle, the size of two fingers. When I put a hand on the deck's floorboards to stand again, I see that the bundle is the hamster. Dead. That's why the cage was outside. Of course.

I lift my hand and wipe the shavings on the thigh of my jeans, look for Russell, then flinch at the porch light's glare. After my eyes adjust, I see that every single one of the fifty people who had shown up are watching me, from the bedroom window, from the yard, from across the deck, from the kitchen door, and Russell is still in the same place, looking dismayed. I meet his eye, breaking some sort of fourth wall, and his mouth closes into a concerned smirk.

I point to the hamster. "It's dead."

• • •

"Do you wanna put your bike in the van, too?" Mason's asking. It sounds like it's not the first time he's said it.

"I wish!"

I'm sitting on the bench seat in Paper Fire's van, the backs of my thighs crinkling into a couple of plastic grocery bags. Lucius is next to me, smelling like powdery artificial strawberry and sick-sweet smoke. Mason and Russell are facing forward, grimly, in the front seat.

**FIVE** On the best nights, shows were a love-
fest with everyone swigging beer with
their arms around each other and chanting "Go go go" between songs.

In the wrong mood, the same show would be a "shirts off,
dudes on" sausage party, the last woman having bolted after getting elbowed by a knot of punk bros.

Save for this really sloppy riot grrrl revival band who played
the bars, there were maybe two women in Richmond punk
bands. And there were a lot of punk bands in Richmond. That's
why I say "guys" and not "people" when I tell you about the
Guys You Don't Want in Your Band:

The Job Guy
Takes his team leader position at the superstore by the interstate
way too seriously. Will cancel practice to bust a shift. Arrives
at shows ten minutes before you're supposed to play and hits
the stage in his work polo, inspiring hecklers to shout stuff like
"Clean-up on aisle three!"

Mr. In Ten Bands
Dude has connections because he also plays with the drummer

from the most popular local band, but you never get to use those connections because he's always practicing with another band. Since everyone sings and plays guitar, this guy is usually a drummer or bassist. Actually, Paper Fire's previous bassist was like that, so Russell and Mason kicked him out. After that, they didn't get asked to play as much, and whenever their old bassist was at a show with the guys from his stupid fake-redneck southern metal band, I could tell he was always just looking at me.

The Skeezeball

Hits on women at every show. Especially young ones, or the promoter's girlfriend. If you haven't seen him for a while, knock before you get your bag out of the van, because you might interrupt a "meaningful conversation."

Too Much Riding on This Guy

Recently single, hates his job, and thinks that ripping off a band he liked in high school will give him purpose in life. Tries to guilt you into thinking your band's career is gonna stall if you can't miss two shifts to play a show in Bowling Green.

The Vegan

Makes you feel bad that there's nothing they'll let themselves eat at the only rest stop in Montana. Meets other vegans and has weird dick-measuring conversations where they point out different things that surprisingly aren't vegan, like "Don't eat that breath mint, dude. It's got gelatin in it. That crap's made from horses." Then they have to make a show of spitting out the mint and glaring at the person they bummed it from.

The Ego

The person who argues until your band gets to play last, or "headline," then gets mad when everyone leaves before you play. The upside of the Ego is that they'll schmooze and wheedle to get your band on shows. The downside is they're too busy schmoozing and wheedling to load the van, and all your friends hate coming to see you play because the Ego refers to them as "fans." OK, that's Mason.

The Shredder

Thinks the best music is the hardest to play. Always tries to solo. Watches instruction videos by famous session musicians. Rolls his eyes at your riffs. Says "four-chord punk" in a tone most folks reserve for "scabies infestation." And this is Russell, a damn good drummer.

The Party Animal

Shouts a bunch. Is too busy drinking beer to load the van. Breaks stuff. Gets too drunk and ruins—ah, crap, this is me.

SIX   That spring, I'd biked past a fistfight outside the grade school. Two nine-year-old white boys in boxy and bright kid clothes tangled their bodies like wire coat hangers while a little brother screamed "Scott!" until his voice broke.

The violence took a moment to register, then I was sickened. One boy was red in the face, teeth clenched, left arm locked around the other boy's middle, right reaching for the throat. The other was a brown bowl cut rippling as his elbow bent back then pummeled the first kid. Neither showed any restraint.

From the handlebars, Lucius murmured, "Dang."

Down the block, a father dropped his daughter's hand, put a hand to her stomach to say "stay there," and ran at the boys.

I slowed, nodded at the dad, who didn't see me, then watched him reach into the fray as I gawked and rolled past, not a fighter, not a parent, not wanting to touch some kids and get mistaken for a creep.

The little brother's screams scraped into guttural sobs. I started pedaling again. The rest of the street was sunny and undisturbed.

Lucius said, "Good lookin' out, bruh. You were a real hero back there."

———

Over a few days, as I felt a drumroll leading up to Mona's return to work, I thought of her struggling with the attacker, and remembered those two boys fighting. Other times, the image was something vague, like a silhouetted cat burglar with a shiny cartoon knife. That was violence to me: scenes pulled from comics and scary movies.

I'd been a spectator to blackness as well. I'd listened to thousands of albums by black artists, watched black movies, read black authors, and laughed late and loud at black comedians' jokes. I didn't just want to learn from them. I wanted to recognize myself.

SEVEN

It was 9:20 a.m., and suddenly the morning rush was over and the shop was empty, save for this guy with a beard and glasses hunkered over his laptop at a corner table. Reggae boomed from the CD Russell and I had put on to keep us mellow. I was full of adrenaline and espresso and stood by the bus tray, darting my head around at the different messes I needed to attend to. Russell was in the bathroom.

A college-age black couple walked in. The guy was tall and wiry with lighter skin and locks past his chin. The woman was short, dark-skinned, and curvy, wearing a hip pair of wire-framed glasses. She lifted a gold sandal over a white plastic cup lid I'd been meaning to pick up, and I was instantly embarrassed by the puddle of milk next to the pitcher on the bar, the dusting of crumbs under a couple of tables, and the crumpled wax paper on a chair, left over from someone's bagel.

"Sorry about the mess," I said. "Rush just ended."

The guy lifted a hand to waist height and shook his head.

I met them at the counter and they both took in my face, then looked at each other. I wanted to say, "Yes, I'm black," but instead said, "What can I get ya?"

The guy said, "Coffee," which is kinda like saying "I want

pasta" at an Italian restaurant, then gave one-word answers when I asked the standard follow-up questions.

Once we'd settled on what he wanted, I looked to the woman, who said, "Same for me," with a tight smile.

Things felt downright frosty, so I overcompensated by flipping the first paper cup in the air when I pulled it off the stack by the coffee urns, then snatching it out of the air with my left hand and swinging it under the spout to catch the coffee as I pressed the lever with my right.

It's an easy trick to do when you don't think too hard about it, but I got rattled when they didn't smile at my showboating, and when I pulled the next cup, it stuck to the one below it and I flung half a dozen paper cups onto the floor at the couple's feet. They startled and stepped back, and I was fixing to apologize when Russell bumped me with the bathroom door and I staggered two steps to my left.

"Sorry," Russell said to me.

"Sorry," I said to the couple.

I could hear the toilet running in the bathroom as the door closed behind Russell.

"Need me to ring anything up?" he asked.

"Just two coffees," the guy said.

"I need more info than that, man," Russell said to him. "What size?"

Then Mona walked in, looking like a peaceful oasis in all the chaos. She wore a yellow T-shirt I'd never seen before and her hair was down, locks bending on her shoulders, giving her an ever-so-slightly more put-together air than I tended to see at work.

I said, "Mona!" and she maybe sorta waved as the couple turned toward her and took turns hugging her, the woman making sympathetic "Ohh" sounds. Mona smiled back in an out-of-place way.

I poured her usual drink, a 16-ounce light roast, into a go cup, thinking, *What do you say to someone who's been through what she's been through?*

"It's good to see you."

I set the coffee down, smiling.

"Thanks," she mouthed, now flanked by the couple.

There was no bandage that I could see, but upon closer look, her face carried a new tension, cheeks higher, mouth lower.

As I finally poured her other friend's cup of coffee, Russell swooped in and hugged Mona. Her head pressed against his chest but she was stiff, eyes open.

She pulled back and said, "Thanks for coming to see me."

"Of course," he said.

Mona's from a town an hour away called Fredricksburg. I could just see Russell sitting in her parents' gleaming subdivision kitchen, feet away from whatever embarrassing posters hung in her high school bedroom.

She introduced him to her friends, who smiled and shook his hand.

I waved and introduced myself too, and the woman nodded and the guy said, "Yup."

Russell started picking up the cups I'd dropped, while the couple sat at the table closest to the counter, and the guy wiped away some crumbs with a napkin. Mona stayed at the counter and asked, "I was wondering if you could do something for me?"

"Sure." Finally, I could be of use.

She was staring at her hand, resting on the counter by her drink. "The police. They . . . Will you go talk to them?"

"OK?"

"I gave them your number," she said. "Since you were at my house that night." She looked me in the eye for the first time since I'd tried to kiss her.

"Like, if I saw anything?" I asked.

"Yeah." She paused. "They said they might want your fingerprints, too. To help pick out the . . . the man's."

"Yeah, of course," I said. Russell walked past and clapped my shoulder. Beyond Mona, the guy was watching me from the corner of his eye as he stirred his coffee.

"Do they have a suspect or anything?" I asked.

"Not really."

She stood over her friends' table for a few seconds, then they rose and walked out with her while I wondered who knew what and what I didn't.

EIGHT

Lucius was perched on the side of the tub, pointing at my toothbrush. "Better bring that to the police station," he said.

"Shut up," I said. "I just brushed." I buttoned my dad's old dress shirt and remembered being a kid and watching him do the same.

Lucius poked the air and said, "Not for morning breath, bruh."

"What am I gonna do?" I asked. "Cut someone with an Oral-B?"

I pinched the back of my collar in both hands and ran them to the front, creasing it, feeling kinda slick.

"Niggas sharpen 'em on the floor in jail." Lucius scribbled the air. "Turn 'em into shivs."

"Damn."

"You should know this by now," he said.

Now.

My knees splayed out as I pedaled Mason's BMX. Lucius jogged behind in an oversized velour tracksuit. We crossed the bricks of the empty campus, heading downtown. Police are bees.

168 / CHRIS L. TERRY

When they're around, sit still and hope they'll leave you alone. But what if you enter their air-conditioned hive?

"How do you think this is gonna go?" I asked.

"I don't know." Lucius panted. "The cops ever been cool?"

I lifted my elbows. While the breeze dried my pits, I flashed over every broken-up show and skate-spot bust.

"Maybe that DEA cop in Texas?" I asked.

We hit the red light by the cathedral on North Laurel. Lucius stopped next to me, hands on knees, chest heaving. "So, you saying . . . that a cop that . . . pulled you over for outta state plates . . . was coo'?"

"Well," I said. "He told us they get a lot of drug traffic on that road."

Lucius frowned and two perfect lines of sweat raced down the side of his face.

"Remember?" I said. "He got real happy when he found out we had a band, because he liked heavy metal or something."

The cop had twanged, "Aw, y'all play heavy music? I love heavy music."

At that, he'd forgotten to search our van for the weed we'd stuck in the baggy fabric hanging from the ceiling.

"Well, good thing you wasn't ridin' up front." Lucius shook his head. "What woulda happened if y'all was some niggas?"

I wiped Lucius's sweat from my upper lip and flicked it into the crosswalk. He was right. I'd been so happy about not getting the van searched that I didn't think about why it had happened. Was I about to be "some niggas" at the police station?

**NINE** If I was some kind of Black Card–carrying hero, this is how things would have gone with the cops:

As I locked Mason's bike to a parking meter, a busy hip-hop beat, with blaring horns and a fast guitar line, would kick in. I'd stand and face Lucius, who'd be dressed like an '80s rapper in a matching red top hat, shades, tracksuit, and giant clock necklace. We'd nod and pivot 90 degrees on our heels, marching in unison up the stairs and into the station.

In the conference room, Lucius would occupy the patch of carpet between my chair and the floor-to-ceiling window, alternating between bodyguard stance and hip-hop hype-man tactics like strutting, throwing his arms up, and punctuating my answers with shouts of "That's right!" and "He's *the man*, but he ain't *your* man for the case."

I'd leap up, office chair rustling the vertical blinds behind me as I pounded my fist on the table and shouted, "This ain't right. You gotta help this girl."

The detective would be cowed: "But how?"

Me and Lucius in unison: "Catch the guy who did it!"

"But who?" the cop would whine.

And then a forgotten vision would rise up in my brain. I'd pluck a blue marker from the table, bound over to the dry erase board, and draw the trenchcoat-and-fedora crook silhouette from a neighborhood watch sign.

"This guy, Detective." I'd point with the marker then cap it with a pop. "But you ain't heard it from me."

"'Cause he ain't snitching," Lucius would say, then roll the marker across the table to the detective, who'd say, "Why didn't you tell me sooner?"

"I forgot," I'd say, grinning. "I was high that night!"

The detective would break poise to say, "Word. I've been there before," and Lucius would reach in for a high five then pull back at the last second.

The cop would whiff then stare dumbly at his palm and go, "Well, I'm glad you remembered."

Then he'd stand and declare, "To the cruiser!"

And I'd go, "We ain't riding in no cop car," and Lucius would shout, "Nah," and the cop would scurry off to get the bad guy.

By the time Lucius and I turned the corner onto my block, Mona would be sitting on my porch, dressed in the classy summer hat from Zora Neale Hurston's old-timey author photo.

When I walked up to the porch she'd purr, "They arrested him. Now how about that kiss?"

And, as I leaned in under her hat brim, Lucius would slip my Black Card into my pocket then make himself scarce.

This is what happened instead:

I sat in the office chair, blinds slicing sunshine across the conference room table, office AC leaving a sickly metallic taste in the
back of my throat. Lucius hovered by my shoulder, patting my
back, coaching me with whispered advice like, "Don't tell them
nothing extra or they'll think you got something to hide. Liars
always be talking too much."

Detective Harrell, a square-faced white guy with puckered
asshole lips and a brown pair of suit pants, stood between me
and the door and asked, "What did you do after you left Mona's
that night?"

I said, "You don't know?"

"No," he said, fast. Everything about him was impatient.

"I spent the night at the precinct on Meadow Street."

Interest flickered in his eyes. "Why?"

"I ran a stop sign on my bike," I said.

"Don't admit to nothing!" Lucius shouted.

"And the officer *said* I was over the legal limit," I added.

"For alcohol?" he asked.

"Yeah."

There was a slight pause while the detective looked at his
notebook. Then he asked, "Drinkin', huh?" with a new buddy-
buddy tone.

"A little, I guess," I said.

"Mona, too?" he asked, showing some tooth. Mona was
only twenty, so I couldn't say that she was drinking beer.

"I don't remember," I said, shrugging apologetically. Lucius
guffawed and Harrell's face flashed through an instant of prick-
ishness before he fired his drinkin' buddy routine back up.

"Do you know if Mona . . . likes to party?"

Lucius wheeled back going, "Psssh!"

"I don't think so," I said.

The cop stayed quiet. I think both of us wanted to say, "Really?"

Instead, I said, "She doesn't seem wild or anything," trying to sound proper.

Harrell made a note, "And you're sure there wasn't anyone else at her apartment that night."

"It was just me and her until her roommate came home," I said. "Bree."

"He wouldn't even let *me* in!" spat Lucius.

"And you left a few minutes after?" Harrell asked.

"Yes," I answered.

"But you wanted to stay," the detective said. I imagined him using this tone of voice on his wife when he's trying to get sex. It shriveled my balls.

"I mean, sure," I said. "But—"

A woman cop walked in and stopped at the table corner. Her jawline came to a point like the bottom of a heart, and her brown hair reminded me of a Christmas wreath. I made eye contact and nodded. Neither of us smiled.

She said, "I'm Detective Newberry. We called you because we're trying to narrow down just what happened that night at Mona's. Are you willing to take a DNA test?"

All eyes on me.

"Lawyer up, bruh! Get a warrant!" Lucius was hovering by my ear, pounding a fist into a palm. "They gonna put your DNA on a knife and blame you! Like OJ!"

"I'm here to help," I said. I figured it'd be over sooner if I cooperated. "What does a DNA test involve?"

Newberry held up a square plastic bag with a couple big cotton swabs at the bottom. Harrell took an Irish goodbye that sent the plastic bag swinging.

Newberry said, "We'll swab the inside of your mouth with one of these. Then we can pick out your DNA from anyone else's in the house."

"Like figuring out whose DNA is whose?" I asked.

"Yes," she said. "Process of elimination."

I pictured everything in Mona's apartment covered in iridescent green dots of DNA.

Lucius grabbed my arm and tried to pull me out of the chair. "All you did was eat that sushi, smoke some herb, try and kiss her, then get your dumb ass locked up. Why do they need your DNA?"

That wasn't a story I wanted to tell the cops, but it was a whole lot better than "try to kiss Mona, then break in and stab her."

"What did this girl tell y'all?" Lucius asked Newberry.

"That's fine," I said. "When do you want to do the test?"

"How about now?" She held up the plastic bag again.

I smiled and said, "Sure."

Lucius groaned and turned to look out the window, rocking heel to toe, hands stretching pockets.

Newberry stood over me, smelling like thin coffee and sharp perfume. The cotton swab scratched inside my cheek.

Harrell came back and said, "Are you sure that you were detained that night?"

"Yes, absolutely," I said around the Q-tip, and some drool caught in the side of my mouth. The swab gripped the inside of my cheek on the way out.

"We don't have a record of your detainment," said Harrell.

"I was there," I said. The bleach and drunk sweat had lingered ever since.

"Did you get a citation?" Harrell asked, the buddy act long gone. "A ticket?"

Newberry paused in the door and watched us.

"Actually, no," I said. "They just kept me overnight in the precinct."

"They should have given you a ticket," said Newberry.

"I was surprised, too," I said. "But I was ready to leave and didn't ask."

"You remember the officer's name?" Harrell asked.

"Yeah, Donahue," I said. "John Donahue."

Harrell and Newberry frowned at each other.

"We know him, right?" Harrell asked her.

"Yes." She nodded, then flattened a palm by her shoulder. "Beat cop."

"Oh, right." Harrell glared at Newberry's hand and she spirited it away. "Donahue," Harrell repeated, and wrote it down.

At first I thought they were gonna write me a ticket then and there, but instead Newberry asked, "Where did you go after you left Mona's that night?" again and they kept asking questions about my night.

At the end of old cartoons, the screen fills in black, eventually circling the main character's face in darkness. Black out the city, black out Bree, black out the silhouette from the neighborhood watch sign—the only face left was mine.

Process of elimination.

Lucius was bounding back and forth behind me shouting, "He didn't do it! Hey now! He didn't do it!" He stopped behind me and shook my shoulders. "Tell 'em, bruh!"

I didn't want to, because saying it out loud would make it real. And, if they didn't think I did it, saying something would make me seem guilty, but then, as Newberry was scooting her chair back and pushing together a few papers on the table, and Harrell was checking his watch and aiming a shoulder at the doorway, I said, "You know I didn't do it, right?"

And they both froze. Lucius's hand squeezed my shoulder. Then Harrell said, "Why would you say that?"

"Because . . . I . . . You . . ."

They watched me hem and haw.

"Because," I finally said, "you're asking me more questions about where I was than about what I saw."

After a beat, Newberry said, "Well, we'll be in touch if we have any more questions."

The day was 99 percent humidity as usual, my natural habitat. When I straddled Mason's bike, the back wheel dragged off the curb and the metal rim dinged the street. Flat tire. I lifted the bike back onto the curb, saying, "Lucius, I think they think I did it."

It hit me as I said it. My breath got short and I white-knuckled the bike's handlebars and wanted to puke and cry and run away so fast I'd wind up in another dimension.

Lucius didn't look surprised. "You was the only one over there, right?"

Damn.

"Damn."

I started pushing the bike down the cracked brick sidewalk. Lucius strolled next to me.

"You sure didn't, though," he said.

"Right." The sun prickled the back of my neck. "But how can I prove it?"

Lucius said, "Nigga who was over there? We can try, but they ain't gonna forget that."

I was the nigga who was over there. Eventually being in the wrong place at the wrong time is something we all have to deal with.

Us.

A wave of cars passed from behind Lucius and me, stirring up a hot breeze on the one-way street.

"Think Mona thinks I did it?"

"Nigga who was over there," Lucius repeated. "Who knows what she told them."

"She wouldn't assume I did it just because . . ."

Lucius stopped me with a hand on my elbow. I faced him across the bike.

"We cut on the TV and see the same mess as white people," he said. "It gets in our heads, too."

I stared into the lenses of Lucius's dark shades and thought of black stuff, of every shiny and out-of-reach thing in rap videos, and how they never settled right with me. Those things weren't the common denominator.

"Lucius," I said. "I'm black."

He did a slow "Yeah, dumbass" nod. "I been trying to tell you that for a minute," he said, and slapped my shoulder. "Come on . . . brotha."

I started pushing the bike again, a black man pushing a white guy's bike that he'd borrowed without permission. I'd been expecting blackness to give the world a sepia quality of light, for my thoughts to walk through my head with a bop, for a parade to come at Lucius and me against traffic on East Grace Street, with leggy black majorettes and a drum line playing a brassy version of a slick r'n'b song.

But nothing.

We stopped at the corner of Belvidere, the six-lane thoroughfare that divides Downtown and the Fan.

"I've always been black," I said to Lucius. "I just shouldn't ever forget it."

"Oh, they won't let you," he said. "And we shouldn't let them. We always have to push back. Just to be ourselves."

I pushed the bike. "So what's next?" I asked. "Jail for life?"

"Sure hope not," he said.

"One night was too much."

"Mmm-hmm," he said. "Is for most people."

"Those cops didn't say anything like 'Don't leave town,' though."

"This ain't one of your movies," said Lucius. "This is real life."

"True."

The light changed and the air stilled as the cars on Belvidere stopped at the red. Lucius faced forward and something about him felt distant, like a tape that's a dub of a dub, as we trudged toward the fountain at the middle of Monroe Park.

ALTERNATE
ME

**ONE** You needed an identity in middle school. I chose skater, like the rest of the wannabe badasses. It was an easy choice. Bart Simpson skateboarded every week on TV. So did the role-playing-game guys who managed to get girlfriends.

Before skateboarding introduced me to my blackness, it was just an excuse to make the suburbs mine. Every yellow curb was begging for a noseslide. Every parking lot for the zigzagging. Every hill for the bombing, knees bent, fingers resting where grip tape met wood.

Since we were a loud, dirty nuisance, the police took notice. They'd start their sirens and we'd scatter like dropped marbles. Sometimes they'd trap us, creeping up while our wheels roared.

I was caught once, in eighth grade. Since I was too young for an ID, I said I was Kevin Canseco from McGuire Road. Cops like baseball, so they called my bluff: "OK, Bash Brother. Wait in the car."

Outside squeezed down to ear-pressing silence as the door closed, then I watched the two cops search my friends on mute, hoping they'd thrown my board in the front seat.

The ride home was faster than skating but felt twice as

long. The cops ignored me after they got the right address, so I glared at the backs of their army guy haircuts while the radio burbled a static version of their smug drawls. After half a second of feeling gangster, I got mad because I wasn't doing anything wrong, and I didn't think my folks would understand that if the cops didn't.

Waiting to be let into my own house brought me back to when I was too young to have a key. When Mom opened up, her eyes got wide and she said, "Hello?" to the cops.

When the cops said, "Your son . . ." Dad appeared at the door. I'll never forget how he was mad at them, and asked what they were charging me with, what they were *claiming* I'd been doing.

When the cops said I'd been trespassing, my dad said, "In a parking lot? That's a public place."

And they said, "Not if he wasn't parking."

And Dad said, "Are you charging him with anything? Is there a ticket?"

And they said, "No, but—" and he said, "Thank you," then told me to go to my room because he had to think about this.

That year, it started seeming like my world was too big to fit in the house with my parents. I fumed on my bottom bunk, and tried to flip through a skateboard magazine, but the page ripped.

I got in trouble for getting in trouble with the cops: a week off the skateboard. When my folks told me to hand it over, I admitted that I didn't have it. Mom deflated and Dad looked furious again.

A few days later, when it seemed like I'd never have another skateboard, Mom stood in my bedroom door and said, "We're worried about you. What's going on? Something has to change."

"Here's a change: stop worrying."

When the yelling moved into a silence that somehow felt worse, Dad drove me to the grocery store and said, "There are people out there who expect the worst from you because you're black. Like when your mother had to go fight to get you put in a better reading program in first grade. And they'll single you out, like those police officers." He gripped the wheel at ten and two. "And we're lucky because we live in a nice neighborhood, but that means that you've got to be extra careful. You stand out."

I looked at the wood fence we were winding past and wondered if standing out in a nice neighborhood meant you weren't nice.

"But Dad," I said, and twisted my wrist to show its inside, whale-belly pale. "I look like Mom. I skate with white guys who are darker than me."

He was quiet for a while, then ran a yellow light for the first time in his life. Sometimes Mom said things like, "You might look a little different, but that makes you beautiful." Meanwhile, Dad never even tiptoed near race. But as we cut onto the parking lot's rough, unskateable pavement, he said, "You're still black, and you need to act accordingly."

Before, I'd only believed I was black when girls asked if they could touch my hair. At any other moment, I was just sure I wasn't white. Everyone was white in the 'burbs, and I definitely wasn't them. Who else dug through their dad's old 45s to find the funk songs that rappers sampled? Who else watched black movies, wanting to live on a block with shared histories? Who else was alone enough to do that?

Dad and I pushed down the lock buttons as we got out of the car, then he chose groceries in silence—a blue box of spaghetti, a foam tray of ground beef, a jug of Chablis. The cashier was a college-age white guy with a zitty chin. He put his hand over Dad's wine and looked from him to me and back, half smiling, then said, "You're buying this for him."

I looked around like, *Who?*

Dad said, "That's my son."

The cashier smiled more and said, "No."

I turned to my father in confusion.

Even though I was insulted that the cashier couldn't tell that my dad was my dad, I wondered if he was proving my dad wrong. If we don't look like family, and I don't look black, then I don't have to be careful.

This was typical of the mess that white people put black people through. Being black wasn't just having cool old records and curly hair, it was to constantly be in trouble. Not trouble like grounded for a week, but trouble like the water is hotter, and your eyes are stuck open. I'd known that heat ever since—in the nauseous fear I feel whenever I see a cop, in the way I never shout the loudest around a bunch of white people—but never felt it cranked up, never was sure that it was a black heat, until I was walking back from the police station with Lucius and that trip to the grocery store popped into my head for the first time in years.

Dad got his wine, and we drove home in silence because he

was never an "I told you so" type of person, and I knew that if I said anything, I'd be acknowledging something I wasn't ready to deal with. Accepting the truth would have taken away the small freedoms and bits of confidence that I'd been elbowing my way into. The same thing had just happened during my DNA test at the police station. This time, I had to listen.

TWO   One shift earlier that summer, I looked up from the dishes to see Mona talking to a virile, middle-aged white guy in cargo shorts and a tank top, with little bug-eye sports shades on top of his head. I couldn't hear them over the sink, but he was gesturing with his hands in a way that conveyed a big intimacy, like he was used to relating to an audience. I'd seen Mason move in a similar manner onstage, when he was really trying to sell his pseudo-political between-song banter, and get the crowd to "keep resisting, even if your phones are tapped."

Mona nodded at the customer slowly as she bounced a bag of coffee beans in her hands. She'd only been working at the shop for a little while, and I remember this moment because, for once, my brain was on pace with my heart, and as I flashed through this moment of wanting her to look at me instead of this arrogant customer, I understood that I was jealous.

First, I was embarrassed at myself for being so unsmooth. I ran a soapy sponge over a small handful of silverware, trying to deny it, asking myself, "What do I care?"

I cared because that day, Mona had laughed at one of my

dumb jokes in a way that made me believe I could think of more to tell. I cared because she seemed interesting and driven and like she had her act together without being joyless or uptight. She was going places and, that day, I'd decided that I wanted to go too.

I looked closer at Mona, wondering if I was developing a crush on the wrong person. She was still nodding, and her eyes were open just a tad wider than they were when she was talking to me. Mona wasn't really listening to the guy, I realized. She was being sarcastic, pulling a super-subtle version of the face you make at a friend across a boring party. I snorted a laugh, and the forks and spoons clattered into the blue sanitizer rinse. They both turned their heads my way, the customer's hands spread in the air, paused mid-proclamation. I bet he had a cocky saying for when he felt interrupted, like, "I'll wait for you."

He didn't say a word to me, though. I felt robbed of the chance to destroy him with my wit, and smiled and nodded, lifted a hand out of the soapy water for a fast wave, then picked up a mug and started washing it.

He took off a minute later, and I saw him pumping past the window on an embarrassing mountain bike with big shocks, left hand pressing an iced coffee to his handlebars.

Mona stepped over to the espresso machine and gave the grill a wipe with a fresh blue sponge.

"One of my professors," she said.

"Cool," I said. "Looks like the type of guy who mountain climbs in a rain forest."

I looked for her reaction and her eyes were narrow, then

they caught mine and she cracked up. She had a great laugh, where she'd bare her teeth and tip her head back about 45 degrees, like she was enjoying some sunshine.

"Does that even make sense?" she asked.

"It does," I said. "On so many levels."

"Got an A, though," she said, after I put another mug in the sanitizer.

And I caught myself before I called her a nerd, and just said, "Awesome."

A couple beats passed and I scanned over the dishes I had left, swaying to the airy folk CD Mona had put on, being glad to be by her.

"What is International Relations, anyway?" I asked.

"It's the way that different countries and cultures interact," she said. I imagined Mona in a UN meeting, making sure people in starving countries got fed.

"That sounds cool," I said. "And complicated."

"The interesting stuff tends to be," she said.

If complicated stuff is interesting, then the last couple days had been fascinating. I hadn't been arrested, though I thought it could happen at any minute, and alternated between breaking into a clammy sweat whenever I saw a sedan shaped like a police car, and catching myself looking longingly at beautiful things I took for granted: the tree branch swishing across my neighbor's garage roof, the blur of light around a streetlamp, the cover of *BW Goes C&W*.

Mona and I worked together two days after I talked to the

cops. The morning before our shift, I was eager for her to set my mind at ease but worried she'd do the opposite. I got there a few minutes early to eat and was in the café's narrow kitchen—a great place to feel like a goony dude, since you can't walk past someone without freaking on them.

I was gingerly rocking a knife back and forth on top of my overstuffed sandwich when Mona popped in and angled a baking tray into the sink by the doorway, then pumped her shoulder, scrubbing it.

A slice of cucumber fell out of the side of my sandwich. I set down the knife and said, "Mona."

She turned fast, snapping a chain of water into the air. I hopped back.

She said, "God. I can't. I can't even have people behind me."

I took another step back. "Look, the police . . ." I said then paused.

"Did you talk to them?"

"Yes," I said.

Water rattled into the sink.

"Thank y—"

"Have they said anything about what they're looking for?" I asked.

She sighed, looking down at the fridge muck our mop never reached. "Just what I told them."

I picked my coffee up off the prep counter, signaling I was settling in for a story. She turned off the faucet.

"It's good to talk about it," she said. "It helps. Um . . ." and she dove in, eyes passing over me, seeing this happen again in real time.

"After you left, I talked to Bree for a while then went to bed at ten forty-five," she said. "I fell asleep quickly. Then, I remember feeling like someone was trying to shake me awake, and I got scared that I was late for work . . . like I was having a dream about it, and I woke up fast. But the hand wouldn't go away. It was pulling at my underwear."

She picked at her hip with her index and middle fingers. The bell over the door dinged and I watched her eyes follow the sound.

"I'll get it." I stepped forward, scared to pass too close, and was relieved when she slid her butt along the rim of the sink, shifting into the corner and out of the way. The customer was this guy with muttonchop sideburns who worked at the record store and always got a bunch of drinks for his coworkers. We traded discounts.

"Hey, dude," he said to me, then curled his upper lip and bobbed his head to the music. "This Horace Andy?"

"I dunno," I said. "It's some reggae comp."

He nodded to himself. "It's Horace Andy."

I wasn't in the mood to chat, or have a white guy tell me about black music, so I waved my pen and said, "What can I get you today?"

He took a second to look taken aback, then started reading his order off a slip of receipt paper. I plucked it from his hand and blindly started filling cups with coffee and milk. If Russell was here, we'd guess if the record clerk woman with the thrift store soccer T-shirts had ordered the soy mocha or the chai tea. Today, I didn't care. She'd want nothing to do with me.

Muttonchops said something over the screech of the milk

steamer. I looked over my shoulder and shouted, "Huh?" right
as Mona appeared next to me and put a hand on the list that I'd
stuck to the top of the espresso machine.

"I said, what's been up?" asked Muttonchops.

Oh, not much, I thought. Just making your coffee real fast
because I can't stop thinking about a burglar fondling that
woman over there. I had a big crush on her. I think I still do. But
now she might send me to jail.

"Chillin'," I answered.

He left, after giving me a red paper flyer for a DJ night he
was doing at Clover's, this skeevy Irish bar that people called
Cloverdose's. Mona was back at the sink, and I clomped past
her to my sandwich, hoping she'd turn around so I wouldn't
have to think of a tactful way to ask, "So . . . where did we
leave off?"

She cut off the faucet again and stood an arm's length away,
at the end of the prep table by the opening to the café.

"My room sounded different," she said. "Like when a window's open and you can hear more from outside?"

I nodded. The air felt thin.

"Bree wouldn't be trying to take off my underwear, so I just
pushed this guy without looking."

Her voice had turned distant and methodical. "I didn't realize he was up on my bed. He fell off backwards, then got back
up and pushed me back on the bed. So I kicked him then got
up and he grabbed me and we fell against my nightstand." She
reached around and touched the middle of her back, near the
kidneys.

"I started trying to push him out of my room and he—"

She pointed at her right shoulder, near where a tank top strap would go. "Well, he stabbed me, then jumped out that little window into the gangway. It was open. I guess that's why the room sounded different. I guess I'd been yelling, because Bree ran in holding one of the stools from our kitchen. I didn't realize he'd stabbed me. I was just too . . . on too much adrenaline."

She pulled her apron away from her shoulder and grimaced. I stuck my tongue between my teeth and top lip and nodded, realizing my left hand was pressing my sandwich's soft bread.

"Bree called nine-one-one," she said. "And they came and took me to the hospital."

"Jesus," I said. "How long were you in the hospital?"

"One night."

"It must have been hard to come back home."

She paused. "I went *home* for a bit. To my folks'."

"Right," I said, remembering Russell's visit. "That sounds good."

She shrugged. "They want me out of here," she said. "They never really liked Richmond."

"Imagine now," I said.

"Mmm-hmm."

Her voice was quiet, drifting in the coffeemakers' trickle.

"Is Bree OK?" I asked.

"She's scared too."

"Did she get hurt?"

"No."

"What did they look like?" I asked, louder.

"Honestly?" Her lips wriggled into a disgusted shape and she stood in front of the sink, left fingers passing over scratched-up right knuckles. "I don't know if, like, you were on my mind because you'd been over earlier, but the guy was thin and kinda tall and he was black but kinda like—" She pointed at me then caught herself. Her hand dropped and she said, "For a second, I thought it was you."

"Oh—"

"But you'd never do something like that."

She caught my eye, demanding confirmation.

"No. No, I wouldn't. I didn't." And I held her eye and said, "You know that, right?"

The words came hard from the gut, going against my father's example of how to not be an angry black man. I pressed my sandwich into the plate. Mona tensed and rocked forward on her toes, ready to bolt. Then the little bell on the door dinged and she flitted out to the counter.

My lungs were empty. I stared at the oily bubbles on top of my coffee, at the fingerprints in the top slice of my sandwich, and, a few seconds later, heard Three-Piece Tarik go, "Hey there, sister. How you been?"

Their voices murmured under the fridge's motor and I stood there, scared to step out to the counter and have them get quiet, like they'd been talking about me.

Does everyone think I did it?

I glanced over the bins of bread, guessing what Tarik might order, then the fridge motor cut out and I heard Mona say, "Sure not easy."

I stepped out, jabbed my chin at Tarik, and scanned my eyes around the café.

Mona said, "I go back for a follow-up this weekend."

With a grave look on his face, Tarik told me, "Keep an eye on this one."

"Damn right," I spat.

Tarik chuckled sympathetically at me. He had no idea.

One of Mona's sentimental-sounding folk rock CDs came on, and I stood in the kitchen doorway, heart going twice as fast as the music, wanting Tarik to leave. Slowly, thoughtfully, he doctored up his coffee at the milk bar, then sauntered out into the brilliant July day, leaving Mona and me, and a couple laptop types peering into their screens at the wood tables.

I looked to Mona, and hissed over the gray plastic cash register, "Did you tell them you thought I did it?"

She stiffened.

I noticed a small gift box in front of her, with an ornate yellow bow on top. I should have brought her something, like Tarik did. I've never even wrapped a gift.

"No. But . . ." She spoke tentatively. Each word was an extra log in the fire. "They pointed out that . . . you do match the description."

I breathed in. All my life, I've been told I look like other people. It can transfer a celebrity's cool onto me. But it can erase me, or worse, place me elsewhere. I gripped the kitchen door frame, trying to crush it with my hand.

"Thanks a fucking bunch, Mona."

"What? What was I supposed to do?" Her voice was ragged, suddenly loud.

"Not drag me into this."

For a moment, I wished I was white and doing white boy stuff, because trying to get my Black Card back had led me here. I flew back into the kitchen and she took a step after me.

I turned. "I got police asking me all sorts of questions about where I was that night. They think I did it. Every time the mailman steps on my porch, I think it's them coming to arrest me. A car drove by slow in the alley the other night, and I jumped out of bed, thinking about running."

Suddenly tired, I rested a hand on the rim of the sink and drew a breath. "You could have told them I wouldn't have—"

"How would I know?" She cut me off. "You think you've got it bad? At least you're not scared to get in your bed in the first place. How would I know, though? Really." Her eyes were glistening, voice loud and pleading.

One of the customers said, "Umm . . . ?" and we ignored them.

"You come over, you try to kiss me." She pointed at her mouth. "You leave. A couple hours later someone tries to," she mouthed the next word with a hoarse squeak, "*rape* me. In my bed. You were fresh in my mind. You don't think I thought of you? It didn't feel good having the cops bring it up. I'd thought it already but they brought it up and said they could make sure. I can't be sure of anything after all this."

I was quiet. She was right.

"And you send me a text when I'm in the hospital? Russell—" She pointed back at his oven-room hangout. "Russell, who once asked if he could be my 'white chocolate'? He had the sense to come visit me. But I'm supposed to think you're a good guy?"

I pointed to her shoulder and said, "I'm a better guy than whoever fucking did that, but I might be in trouble for it."

Bree walked in wearing a patchwork dress. I scraped my side on the counter as I ducked back into the kitchen, but not before I noted Mona's revolted silence.

I stood stock still, catching my breath, then peered out around the doorway. Mona was grimacing by the register. Bree glared at me through her little oval glasses and asked, "Mona, are you OK with this man here?"

I ducked back into the kitchen. A long block of cream cheese softened on the prep table next to my sandwich. I decided to leave it for Mona to portion.

 Alternate Me. Ever-so-slightly darker. Not "me in July after a couple trips to the river" darker, but naturally darker, so there's no doubt about his blackness.

Alternate Me. Doesn't walk so stiff. Kinda rolls. Has a muscley stomach so he doesn't suck it in and walk like it hurts. Might flex his chest and shoulders, but his gut is in, and his butt is out, with a white puff of boxers above his jeans. His sneakers are clean. They aren't some raggedy skater ones covered in coffee grounds.

Alternate Me. Desperate for something to turn his life over, push it forward and make him more than the nobody alone in his room, solo on the sidewalk while everyone tells him he looks like someone else. While no one sees him just for him. Just sees a random rapper, actor, singer, light bright 'n' almost white brother useta go to Ebenezer Baptist Church before the preacher started asking for money instead of sharing about Jesus. This guy who broke into my place and tried to rape me.

Me with a name, I guess. Him with one too. But neither of them mattering, because we're so many other people.

We're satellites. People's vision bounces off of us. The reflections glare in their eyes.

Every time someone played the "You Look Like" game, Alternate Me and I overlapped, until we went in different directions, picking up steam and a need to blow it off. I'd picked up a bass guitar and an ear for white boy music. Had he picked up a knife?

If I knew his street, I could've walked down it and been him. Had he beaten me to it? Had he walked down my street and been me?

And now I was nobody, alone in my house, watching smoke spin off an angry '70s soul record and swirl above the record player. Taking that first sip of beer two-thirds down the bottle where it's more warm than cold. Quiet, thinking, *I could have been the one in Mona's apartment. He could have been the one onstage or at the café.*

I could see myself as a dotted outline holding a bass in front of my amp while Mason and Russell played. I tried to envision Mona's apartment in the middle of the night, like in an old horror movie where the camera shakes while they do the killer's-eye view.

All of my furniture disappeared and my butt thumped to the floor. Once I caught my balance, I saw that the living room was bare, except for me, the beer bottle that had splashed onto my hand, and particles of dust twisting in the stuffy air.

Kids played outside, muffled through the closed windows. A woman shouted to someone. They all sounded black.

"Aye, in here, bruh," Lucius called from what should have been my room.

On my way in, I looked to the left and saw an empty dining room. Down the hall, a dim kitchen with black and white checkered tiles.

My bedroom was the same size, and smelled faintly of dandruff and weed. A '70s-looking round orange lamp on the floor compensated for the heavy curtain someone had hung over the window under the stairs, and was replicated in miniature on the lenses of Lucius's plastic aviator shades. He sat in the middle of the bed, feet on the floor, facing the window in basketball shorts and a black tee.

The door closed behind me. A bassy car stereo rumbled past, drowning out the calls of kids down the block. A strange dresser, made from scarred wood, stood where mine should have been.

Lucius spread his hands. "It's like you're home already. You know this, right?"

I nodded because it seemed like my apartment, or one of the many similar ones around town.

Lucius pointed at the lamp on the floor between us, and with the ghost story light illuminating his chin, he asked, "Is this old thing cool?"

"Nah."

My punk friends would never admit to wanting nicer, newer stuff. I always sorta did. Convincing yourself you like the only thing you can afford is a survival tactic, but not necessarily cool.

"Exactly." Lucius nodded. "It ain't cool, but it's life."

I smiled at the truth.

"You want this life to be yours?" Lucius asked, pointing his shades at me.

"What life? The stabbed Mona life? The empty-ass apartment life?" I asked.

"The black life," Lucius snapped. "I made this place for you."

I took a step in. "Dude. This is my apartment."

"It could be," Lucius said. "It's your fresh start. Go out on the porch and see. You're in Church Hill now."

One time, my old roommate's fat gray tabby cat ran away. A week later, I found it in a neighbor's garden and carried it inside, so proud of myself for doing good by my roommate. As I unlocked our front door, the cat felt odd in my arms, like a week on the street had changed its size. But it wasn't until I set it down on our kitchen floor and it hopped onto the table and cowered, hissing at me, that I realized it was a different cat.

As I walked back through the empty living room, this apartment didn't hiss, but it had a similar feeling of being so damn close, but inherently different.

The sun hit my porch from a new angle. Out front was an older road with a hump of pavement in the middle. An old lady sweeping a porch across the street nodded to me. I stepped onto the sidewalk and a handful of little kids ran around me laughing, and I found myself feigning friendly punches at them, then even fist-bumping a guy in a turquoise baseball cap who leaned out the window of a passing Plymouth. Everyone was black. The street felt alive.

My usual block was dead, empty and white. Some old guy had even threatened to call the cops when I was throwing my thrashed sneakers over the power line after the Paper Fire tour. There were no daps there.

I smiled to myself and walked back across the porch, turning around for one last look before going inside and straight to my room.

"Just like that," Lucius said. "You just gotta let everything go to do it. You can be that Alternate Me."

I felt my stomach sucking in, my army shorts snaking down my butt, and a waft of cool air as my boxers lifted away from the top of my butt cheeks.

"Finally," Lucius said.

"But I've already got a life," I said.

"But it's white."

"But I like it."

"You like being white?" Lucius asked.

"I'm not white," I said. "I thought we figured that out."

In North Carolina, I'd been jealous of all of Richmond, scanning my mind over every lit-up window in the city, wondering which one had Mona hugged up on some guy behind it.

In Richmond, I'd been jealous of every bohemian-looking black dude: the guy with thick glasses and holey jeans who worked at the health food store; the guy with the Converse and camera who came to shows every now and then; the dude with the locks who'd been in that group art show, standing self-assured by an earth-toned painting. They could all offer something to Mona while I'd wanted to take: her blackness, her sex, her homespun sushi, her easy confidence.

In Richmond, I'd been a moth. I'd fluttered, rising and bumping the ceiling, orbiting in Mona's glow, never quite settling.

But the minute Mona told the cops about me, she'd given me something. She'd made it so I'd never, ever doubt that I was black, no matter where I was.

"I've always been black," I told Lucius. "White mom or not."

A breeze ruffled the heavy curtain.

"That's true," Lucius said. "But you could always be blacker. You could take this new life, for insurance."

"But what would I do here?" I asked. "The life I've already got is black because I'm living it."

Lucius squeezed his forehead with thumb and pointer and nodded in surprised agreement.

"I been living it, Lucius," I said. "I'm done trying to catch up when I'm already running."

As I turned heel and bolted out the door, I think I heard him murmur, "My nigga."

My knees straightened with each footfall across the porch, forcing away the b-boy limp that had started seeping in.

"Now you're literally running from being black." Lucius's voice was in my head.

"So, wait, *was* that you? It *wasn't*." Mona joined him up there.

"You're under arrest." Donahue in unison with Newberry, who'd lost her bedside manner.

I stood on the sidewalk in front of this new house, scanning every porch, face, and car hood in sight, waiting for someone to tell me to stick around.

Silence.

I was alone, the only time I can be exactly who I feel like being. A time that raises the question: If a black man does something and no one sees it, how can he know if what he did was black?

I sat down on the stoop. Night fell and the street grew quiet. Memories tossed in the air and landed in a new configuration. Black. Black. Black.

Black Dad in our black Volkswagen, telling me that people automatically assume the worst about my black ass . . . not just a family moment, a black family moment.

The police detective, swabbing for black DNA . . . not just cops, cops against brothers.

Black Mona at the gleaming black sink, telling me the black guy was light skinned and my height . . . not just a black suspect, but a police sketch that we all sorta look like.

My favorite bass line was in my head, the unforgettable descending one from "Pusherman" by Curtis Mayfield, written and played by a black man. It was joined by skittering congas and guitar, Curtis's soulful and tender falsetto, all produced by black people.

I wiped sweat from my upper lip, remembering my father, careful as can be, easing the black vinyl disc out of the black paper sleeve with the little Buddha on it, then holding it by its edge and placing it on the turntable.

Remembering eighth-grade me, zitty in baggy, plaid pants, letting that bass line slink into my head while I was walking up the hill from the bus stop, or tempering my hormones by tapping on the armrest of our car.

That riff being one of the first things I picked out on the bass, figuring out that first note, then the second and third, plunging along with it, tingling with discovery as I completed the melody.

It was black people listening to black music. I was a black person playing black music. My experiences were black, even though they weren't the ones I'd seen on TV and pieced together for Lucius.

MAGICAL
NEGROES

 **ONE** The following people are racist:

White guys who get too happy when they're singing along with a rap song and the emcee says the n-word.

White guys who think Outkast say "ghetto belts and patty melts," not "gator belts and patty melts," at the beginning of "So Fresh, So Clean," because white people say the word "ghetto" all the time and associate it with blackness, so why wouldn't a rapper use something called a ghetto belt to keep up their pants?

Those same white guys who think 1970s pimps with huge feathered hats and purple flared suits are hilarious and amazing, but don't realize that a gator belt is some pimp shit that'll match your gator shoes (and we've gotta use the whole gator). And who don't care that a pimp is a leech, and that to glorify a black pimp is to make light of violence against black women.

Those same white guys who think pimps are cool, and song after song about gun violence is cool because they're removed from it. They don't have to worry about whose funeral is next, or if it might be theirs.

Anyone who thinks that the only examples of racism are the extreme ones, like Nazis, Klansmen, and people who don't just say "nigger" but "I hate niggers."

White people from the suburbs who think that everyone from the city is black, and make comments about it when they head into the city to do white people activities like come to my job for a latte.

White punk rockers who think they're ending racism by forming an antiracist organization with a dozen other white folks.

Black people who do the white guy voice.

White people who do the black guy voice.

Half-white guys who get way into punk rock as a reaction to their black classmates not being into skateboarding.

No DNA results that I knew of. No arrest yet. Lucius sat on the couch and slowly stretched his neck while I did twenty more push-ups inside the square formed by the stereo, couch, love seat, and pushed-aside coffee table. My shoulders and neck burned. Prince cranked on the stereo and I resisted the urge to hump the floor with each push-up.

1 . . . 2 . . .

"We could just call the cops and ask to speak to Donahue. Ask him to send the ticket so we have proof," I told Lucius.

3 . . .

"Boy, brothas don't call the cops," he said.

4 . . . 5 . . .

Sunlight made the curtain on the front door glow.

. . . 25.

I dropped to the floor, scraping grit onto my sweaty cheek.

"Why do you always listen to this old-timey music?" Lucius asked while I stood up.

"I like it," I said, stretching my neck away from my shoulder. "I came up on it."

He dropped to the floor and got in plank position. "Your

pop was just as likely to throw on some rock 'n' roll nonsense."
He grunted and rose up.

I laughed. "That's true."

He sighed, flattened to the floor, and said, "I don't hear you
throwing on that 'money for nothing and the chicks for free,'
song, though."

I exhaled. "That song *is* a joint. You're right."

I started air-guitaring and singing the riff, *Dudda-lit nuh-
hh-nit nuh-nit nuh-nit.* Lucius laughed mid-push-up and crashed
to the floor, then joined in, slapping out the beat on the floorboards like a wrestling ref, singing in an extra nasal voice. I
started jerking my arms like a wind-up soldier.

My phone buzzed on the coffee table and the screen lit up
green.

> From: Mason
> 10:48 am
> *Katis show at 7*

> To: Mason
> 10:49 am
> *See you there*

Lucius appeared next to me and stirred sugar into his mug,
the spoon making a pleasant ding on the porcelain.

"That's them fools from North Carolina, right?" he asked.

"Yup," I said.

"Do another set." Lucius pointed to the floor. "Gotta get
your front up for the white boy brigade."

I bent my knees and put my palms to the floor then asked, "I can't turn being black off and on, right?"

"Nope." He sank back onto the couch.

"Well, they can't turn my black off either," I said. "Just you watch."

THREE

Mason couldn't find a regular venue for Kill All Their Infernal Soldiers and their unwieldy band name to play. Russell agreed to put on the show in his basement, where we practice. We passed out some flyers, left messages on a few punk-house answering machines, and Mason posted about it on some message board. We figured that if Russell's roommates and their assorted girlfriends, boyfriends, and drinking buddies watched, the basement would be full. After the amps, drums, and clogged washing machine, ten's a crowd down there.

That's why Lucius and I were so surprised when we walked up the alley behind Russell's three-story row house to find a dozen punks moving out of the way so that two cars with North Carolina plates and a bunch of equipment in their back windows could park by Russell's basement door.

"People like their band?" Lucius asked, confused.

"I don't think anyone's heard of them," I said.

If you're playing, it's a great feeling to walk up to a crowded show. I was a little scared to be out of the house but still excited. Tim from KATIS stepped out of his hatchback, grinning and slowly turning to take in the small crowd.

Lucius and I walked up, brushing the warm hoods of

KATIS's cars until we got to Russell, who was sitting on the back steps drinking a can of beer, which he tucked behind his butt when he saw me.

KATIS's quiet drummer, who looked to be younger than me, walked up first and waved even though he was so close he almost slapped Lucius. Then JJ sidled up, jaw doing an "I've got reason to be embarrassed but I'm gonna get defensive if you push it" wiggle. Finally, Tim joined us, carrying his guitar case and saying, "This is already great! . . . Is our stuff OK in our cars?"

It's a question that we ask in almost every town we play. Still, I hate it when people come here and assume they're gonna get broken in on.

"Hopefully," I said.

Tim tightened his grip on the guitar case. Behind him, that girl with the super-sculpted eyebrows caught my eye and air-guitared, then toppled backwards while her friends laughed.

"What happened?" Tim asked.

"I got drunk and messed up our last show."

"Yeah, that," Russell agreed.

"Ha, tight," said JJ, and Lucius and I mean-mugged him. His jaw went back to quivering.

The plan was that KATIS would go on first in case the cops came. Plus, we wouldn't have to move our equipment after we played.

While his bandmates were stretching their legs after the drive, JJ pointed his chin at me and said, "Can we talk?"

Lucius and I followed him across the back porch, walking

through this pack of sketchy skaters who always come to shows but never watch the bands.

Inside, JJ stood in front of the range and asked me, "Are you pissed about my family?"

I propped a hand on the counter by the sink full of dishes and slowly leaned, watching him squirm.

"Why would I be pissed?" I asked, quiet and calm, setting him up to say the n-word. By the fridge, Lucius snorted a laugh.

"Because of what they were saying." JJ looked out the window over the sink.

"I thought all you white people talked like that," I said.

"I don't!" he pleaded.

"Bet you did at one point," I said, standing up straight. JJ flinched, ever so slightly.

Lucius clapped his hands together and backed me up with a "Mmm-hmm."

"Bet when you were a kid you said it at the wrong time and your dad gave you a talkin' to," I said. "About how it's a word y'all just use at home."

JJ looked everywhere but in my eye. I wished the fan above the stove would suck him up and away.

Lucius said, "Gotcha."

"But," I continued, "after a while, I bet you realized it wasn't cool to ever talk like that."

JJ said, "Yeah, and they won't listen to me. It sucks, dude." He took a deep breath and added, "You musta been pissed."

"I was, and not just because I'm black," I said. "My white bandmates didn't like it either."

I wanted to say that I felt bad for not saying something that night, and that we can't control our families, but then he leaned in, squinted at me, and said, "Wait, did you just say you're black?"

I'm giving a test every time I put my black identity out there, by doing something as direct as saying "I'm black," or as ordinary as listening to rap music in public. The only way to pass is to be black and approve, or to be white and just not say anything.

I fail when black people get skeptical.

White people fail by criticizing or questioning me, and blackness in general.

JJ failed.

Lucius grabbed my shoulder and said, "I know you're about to break out that family photo."

I'd spent a few years carrying a photo of my folks and me in my wallet. My grandpa took it on his porch during our first Thanksgiving in Richmond. I'm standing in the middle in the one sweater I owned at the time, and there are invisible arrows from my father's half smile to mine, my nervous eyes to my mom's.

I told myself lots of people carry family photos, but I'd only bust that one out when someone didn't believe I was black. I hated how well the photo worked. If I was always so ready to provide evidence, it proved the point of the people who didn't believe me. Besides, I knew who I was.

"I'm done using a picture to prove it," I said.

JJ said, "Picture?"

"Picture?" I said. "Never—"

A guy in a denim vest marched in, said, " 'Scuse me," and hit JJ in the butt when he opened the oven door to pull a beer from a twelve-pack he'd stashed in there. Lucius and I took this opportunity to snake through the house's dim bottom floor and out onto the empty front porch.

We stood in the dark and watched cars pulling into the strip mall across the street, where music and voices spilled out from a trendy-looking restaurant.

Tim and KATIS's drummer appeared at the corner to our left and sauntered across. I watched, jealous of how natural they looked, like this city had been built for them, and they could keep going and weave themselves into it, becoming two more white boys with pickup trucks and golden retrievers they take to the river each weekend.

Tim went into the convenience store next to the bar and the drummer stood outside, shuffling from foot to foot with his phone wedged between his ear and shoulder. A cop car glided up to the curb on our side, with its spotlight shining on Lucius and me. Was this it? I flinched away from the glare.

The cruiser stopped in front of a fire plug. The doors opened and a tall cop with see-through blond hair, a short chin, and a tiny mouth got out of the passenger side. The sinking feeling that started when they rolled up kept sinking when John Donahue stepped out of the driver's side, a black hole in the summer night. As they walked up, Donahue talked out the side of his mouth into his shoulder microphone and peered around at the street, the sidewalk, and us on the porch.

He stopped with a foot on the bottom step, his partner standing up straight in the middle of the sidewalk behind him, and asked, "This the party? Got a call sayin' . . ."

When he recognized me, he broke his cop cool with a double take then said, "You? Of course you're here," as he barreled up the stairs. His partner put a hand to his holster and ran after him, their footsteps like a thunderstorm. They were on us before we could bolt for the door or hop off the side of the porch.

"We got some talkin' to do," Donahue said, gathering my arms behind my back and pulling me toward the stairs.

"We do it here?" I asked as cuffs click-click-clenched my wrists and my head lurched out over the staircase. Donahue pulled me back and scoffed.

"Lucius!" I called.

"I'm here, bruh. Ain't much I can do."

"Forget it, bud," Donahue's partner said in a guttural mountain accent.

I tried to turn and look for Lucius but Donahue yanked me forward and we trotted down the stairs to the cruiser. I caught a brown-haired yuppie woman in an SUV across the street staring and she turned away.

Some punks walking up to the show paused on the sidewalk as the cops pushed me into the back seat. By the time I'd righted myself, they'd walked on, faster. Lucius was a shadow on the porch, standing stock still between the living room window and front door. The cruiser's front doors slammed, then Donahue whooped his siren and sped into traffic. The cuffs dug into my wrists as I pressed into the seatback.

"I didn't get a ticket that night," I shouted at the little holes in the plexiglass.

Donahue slammed on the brakes at the red light on the corner, said, "You can't go telling my police business," then cut a right turn. "Trying to get an officer in trouble isn't gonna get you in any less trouble," he shouted over the engine.

"What trouble?"

We took the next right and I rolled against the door. His partner just kept looking forward, silent. Donahue took a left then a right into the alley, toward the geometric park. He stopped on the cobblestones and turned around.

"Don't play stupid with me." He shook his head. Through the windshield, the little alley park's light gray concrete structures glowed in the moonlight. "I know what's going on with that black girl at your stupid Generation X job."

"I was locked up when she got attacked," I said, trying to stay calm. His partner looked over his shoulder at me, still creepy and impassive. "You locked me up. And I don't have a ticket."

"Yeah, you're welcome," he said. "I tore it up after I dropped you off. Wish I hadn't. I've been catching a world of shit for that."

With that, he threw his door open, walked around the front of the car and opened my door, "Get out."

I stumbled on a cobblestone then faced Donahue, who spun me by the wrist and took off the cuffs. The park was empty and quiet, save for the hum of the cruiser's engine behind me and the crunch of my sneaker in the pebbles as I turned back around. Streetlights sprinkled through the trees, casting the bottom half of Donahue's face in yellowish light as he reached for his belt and I flinched. No bang, no pain. He pulled off his holster and dropped it and the cuffs on the car trunk.

I waited for him to speak as he stepped back to me. He shifted his weight then a white fist appeared in the dark a foot from my face. Stars dripped from the night and my tailbone found an extra pointy rock to land on.

It happened so fast that heat, snot, and tears were still rushing to my cheek and eye when he said, "Get up," then immediately reached for me, hooked a hand under my armpit, and pulled me forward.

"Stickman, wannabe, all sorts of shit." Donahue was fighting back a yell. "Black people called me that. Still do."

My balance was off. A fist I never saw crushed into my gut. As I folded, that first fist popped me again and I fell, reeling sideways this time, landing in a fetal position with my butt pointed at Donahue, who kicked it hard enough for me to skid a couple of inches across the ground, thankfully away from him.

His shadow fell over me and he said, "Got called nigger-lover for listening to rap, too."

I wheezed. It felt like his fist had lodged itself in my lungs.

"You didn't," kick in the shin, sharp pain up my leg with an undercurrent of ache in the bone, "have," kick on the outside of my thigh, right on some tendon that sent razors coursing down to my knee, "that." A heavy shoe came to rest on my side, between ribs and hip.

"Fuckin' loved Wu-Tang," he muttered.

I knew I could stand but I wanted it to be over and hoped lying still would help. He jostled me and it would have tickled if everything else didn't hurt so much.

"Get up."

I sighed and went limp.

He flicked me onto my back with the same shoe. "Get up."

He knelt by me. To someone at the mouth of the alley, it might look like he was helping a passed-out homeless guy.

"You had so much and you wasted it."

His hand snaked between my right side and the ground and he wrapped a hand around my puny upper arm and pulled me sideways. Beyond him was a knee-high concrete ledge, then the small brick park with a concrete climbing structure that looked part art and part playground. His partner leaned against the passenger door, watching us with hands on hips.

"Wasted your black." Donahue shook his head, backlit. With a grunt, he stood and pulled me up with him.

"You coulda done more," he said.

"I coulda faked it?" I slurred, wavering back and forth.

"Hmm?" He cocked an ear at me, so sure I wasn't going to hit him. I wanted nothing more than to do it.

"Nothing," I said, spitting and falling toward him.

He took a quick half step back like a country line dancer and my face met his fist when I was at a 45-degree angle from the ground. I twisted and dropped.

"Try to help you out and this is how it goes," he said. "Stay down. And you don't wanna go back into that party, because I'm about to."

I took a long blink then a quaking breath. A car door slammed and an engine revved and I lay there near the little wall, feeling like I had a dozen hearts beating double time in each place where he'd hit me or I'd hit the ground.

**FOUR** Back in high school, John Donahue would say "nigga," like black people do, not "nigger" like his parents said.

Lying on the ground after Donahue took off, I remembered a time at school when he shouted it at a black buddy of his named Kevan. Those two were like a tumbleweed of violence, taking up more space than their two bodies should need, constantly in motion, shooting cartoon lightning bolts.

After a couple weeks of shoulder checks and a "what you lookin' at," I smartened up and would literally turn around and go the other way if I saw them. I'm not proud of that, but I am cool with not getting my ass kicked.

This day, it was too late. They were across the hall, and a few people were between us so I didn't see what happened, but I heard the boom of a kid slamming into a locker and immediately tensed as my internal John Donahue alarm went off.

The hall held its breath, waiting to see if there was gonna be a fight.

Then it came—"Daaamn, nigga!"—in Donahue's white southern accent, made hoarse by being forced into sounding like a cartoon version of a black person.

I wondered if Donahue paused before it, asking himself if it was a good move.

I wondered if he sneakily cocked an ear after, hoping no one reacted, and that his nigga landed naturally.

It didn't. A black guy with a bald fade bopped Kevan's shoulder and pointed at Donahue. Kevan pursed his lips. Donahue rubbed his shoulder and popped a sheepish "Come on, guys" grin, a new look for him. Then Kevan shook his head and said, "Naw."

"What?" asked Donahue. He knew.

"Nigga," said Kevan. "Don't say that. White people don't say that."

A couple chins went up, starting to nod in agreement, and I heard the "mmm" part of an "mmm-hmm," but it got cut off when Donahue shouted, "But I'm not white!"

And whatever Kevan said next was drowned out by laughter, from the smart couple who dressed like adults and sat dead center in Honors English, and the funny guy from the football team who'd always sneak into my art class to see his girlfriend, to Kevan's friend who I once saw standing topless in the hall next to the vice principal, turning his yellow Phillies Blunt T-shirt inside out before putting it back on.

It took a moment of watching the kids slapping their knees and turning away with fists balled to their mouths before I understood that, this time, the derisive laughter was not directed at me. I joined in, even though I'd sworn I never would because I knew how bad it felt to be on the receiving end. But I hooted, and put a fist to my mouth too, and looked over a girl with a pixie cut's shoulder until Donahue's eyes locked onto mine, and I just kept forcing out the laughter until my cheeks ached and he looked away.

FIVE

Leaning against a brick wall looks cool on a record cover, but it's scratchy and uncomfortable in real life. The wall I was leaning on belonged to the bar across from work. I was looking at a smudge of light in the coffee shop's oven room. It was 3:30 a.m. My entire body was stiff from being beaten up. I'd stayed in the alley for a few minutes then spent a couple hours zigzagging the neighborhood's alleys before going home, where I'd discovered that it hurt to lie in bed.

I walked across the blue-dark patio. When I unlocked the café door, Russell peered out from the oven room and said, "Little late for the show, dude."

I stopped at the counter. "Wait, this isn't the venue?" He didn't laugh, so I added, "I'm sorry."

He stepped into the doorway, frowning, sleepy. "What the hell happened to your face?"

"Would you believe that I got punched by a cop?" I realized I was slurring.

"What?" He slapped the door frame.

I nodded.

The oven timer buzzed.

"Hold on." He disappeared into the oven room. I stepped around the counter and followed him into the small orange-walled room that was twenty degrees hotter than the rest of the café. He was sliding a muffin pan onto the cooling rack. I reached onto the shelf below it and grabbed a hot biscuit, half of which I crammed in my mouth. The biscuit was like five saltines at once. It had been hours since I had any water. Plenty of beer, though, mostly drunk in the other alley park, over off Strawberry Street.

"We were worried." Russell pursed his lips and dialed up the heat on the oven. "Man, they really got you. What did you do?"

"Nothing," I said with a thick tongue. "Why does it always have to be what I did?"

"What the hell is going on with you these days? Are you in trouble?"

"I hope not," I said. "It's not my fault. Don't—look, I'm sorry I've ruined the last couple shows," I said, stopping short of promising to do better.

"Whatever to that." He waved a hand. "Look, man, I heard you got into it with Mona?"

"I think she thinks I did it," I said.

A big crumb of biscuit fell to the floor and I stooped to pick it up, then popped it in my mouth.

"Well, you didn't, right?" he asked.

"No, dude! Why would you even think that?"

That same crumb, now wet, flew onto the toe of Russell's sneaker.

"I don't know." He shook his head and looked at his shoe. "I've never . . . this has never happened. I don't know what to think."

"But you knew to sneak off and go visit her."

"Sneak?"

"I woulda come."

He shrugged. It seemed dumb to compete over Mona now.

"Uh, what did she tell you? About when we got into it?" I asked.

"That you talked to the cops, then got mad at her. Uh," he pointed out the doorway behind me, "would you hand me a napkin?"

He followed me out to the area behind the counter, the floor hard without the usual no-slip rubber mats. He used the napkin to pick at his shoe, trying not to smear the biscuit crumb into the suede. "If you didn't do it, you'll be fine. Quit acting like the world's out to get you."

"It's been feeling like it is," I said. "Maybe it's never felt like that for you."

He paused, crumpled the napkin, "No, but still. Don't let that affect your job. And your band."

"Russell." I pointed the biscuit at him. "You got the cops in your face? You being suspected of a crime you didn't do?"

"No," he said. "But it—"

"Don't say it," I said.

"Say what?" He pointed the palms of his oven mitts at the ceiling.

"Don't say it's Black Stuff."

He turned his palms toward me and said, "I wasn't gonna."

Most of me believed him, but I still turned and walked out, trailing biscuit crumbs to the door and thinking about how he would have been right if he had said it, but wrong for saying it if he did.

**SIX**

It had been a week since I skipped the show. My worn family photo sat in its new home on my dresser, under the stolen pint glass where I saved quarters for laundry. I hadn't seen Lucius. At the shop and at the one show I went to, people would wince when they saw my face, then ask, "How's the other guy look?"

I got sick of the awkward silence after I said, "Like a cop," so I'd been hiding out at home or going on long walks toward the city's western edge while the black eye lightened to a green caterpillar crawling up my face.

Mason had blown off my apology with a "That's OK," touched the handlebars of his bike before glaring at the flat tire, then slunk off to his girlfriend's on foot.

Similar reaction from Russell, but sub in scrubbing under the prep fridges at work, which I suspected he was doing to avoid me. No one would do that for fun.

They couldn't help me, but I still wanted more from them, be it a cussing out, or one of those over-the-top laugh sessions we used to have in the van.

There were so many things I wanted to forget, pick apart, or talk smack about. No one was there to hear them and I just felt like screaming at someone, a funky James Brown scream, not a punk singer one.

Pretty sure Mona had switched some shifts to duck me as well, so this was our first time working together since the punch. She glanced at the remnants of my black eye, but we didn't speak for the first couple hours, save for work stuff that felt robotic and overly polite. "Yes, I will make her mocha. Was that no whip?"

Mona was at the counter, paying too much attention to wiping it off, again. I came out of the kitchen, drying my hands on my apron, and said, "Hey. I'm sorry about the other day. I got scared I was gonna go to jail or something."

She nodded. "I see that. You were trying to help by talking to them, then . . ."

"Yeah," I said. "Made me wonder just why they wanted my DNA."

"Look," she said. "If I really thought you did it . . . would I be right here right now?"

My mind whirled. She was right, but she wasn't the police.

She walked into the kitchen, shaking her head. I started after her, and the shop door opened to let in this plumber that we call 'Preciate-it Man, because that's what he always says. I poured his iced tea so fast it splashed on the counter, handed him the dripping cup, and said, "This one's on me."

By the time he said "preesh," I'd followed Mona into the kitchen. She was standing there, staring down at the prep table.

She looked up and faced me. She wasn't crying. "I don't need this shit."

I rocked on my feet, stepping toward her then leaning away,

and settled a couple steps back, butt on the edge of the dish sink, eye on the counter. The bell over the door rang as 'Preciate-it Man left.

"Any progress?" I asked her. "Like, with the cops?"

"No. When they came in that night . . . *that night* that night?" She stared at the wall, "They saw the pipe on the coffee table."

"Oh."

"They're treating me like a drug addict," she hissed. "They're asking me all these questions like 'Do you ever have strangers over to get high?' and 'How often do you party?'"

When she said "party," I remembered Detective Harrell's creepy tone.

She took two slices of wheat bread out of the bag above the prep table. "It's like they think that smoking a little weed made it *my* fault," she said. "They just . . . seem to think it's why *it* happened." We both watched the coils in the toaster oven turn orange. "The people you think are gonna help you?" she said. "They never do."

 **SEVEN**

After my shift with Mona, I got sick of sitting at home and went to a party alone. After standing outside for a couple minutes, looking up and down the street to make sure the cops weren't rolling up, I found myself in a muddy backyard, sipping beer in a circle near a younger guy who had the enthusiasm of a new drinker. He kept smiling with his mouth open and clapping my back. Each time his palm landed, my shoulders would rise and my eyes would narrow a bit more. Across from me was a woman with big eyes, smelly armpits, and a welcoming air. She used to date one of Russell's roommates and was friendly enough to talk to and good-looking enough to linger around. To my right was one of her friends, who kept staring over our heads at the other clusters of partygoers.

The new drinker guy clapped my back again. I shut my eyes and took a slow breath, listening to the last half-inch of beer lapping up the inside of my can. Then he asked, "Did you quit Paper Fire?"

I winced. "No, I just. No." I rubbed my chin with my thumb, two-day stubble scraping like skateboard grip tape. "Had a couple tough shows."

"Ha! Yeah, at the Dog Day Afternoon show, you were like,"

and the kid did an impression of me that started off as a flailing air guitar shimmy and turned into a stumble that kicked up chunks of wet dirt and grass. Smelly Armpits and her sour-faced friend stepped out of the way.

I was relieved that word hadn't gotten around about me getting taken away by the cops, but I wondered, is this my life? Getting clowned by a white kid who's younger than me?

"Yeah." I laughed and agreed and hoped the embarrassing story would go away faster.

The kid stood up. "Anyway, you guys rock." He flashed the cheesy pointer-and-pinkie devil horns. "I was just wondering because, like, who was that guy playing bass for your band the other night?"

"Huh?"

"They played a couple songs, but with another bassist," he said, scissoring his fingers, playing air bass.

"Oh, I didn't know that," I said.

"Yeah," he said.

I shook my beer can. "I'm gonna get some more."

"They're out," said the woman who didn't want to be there.

I felt like a ghost stuck haunting a past life. A past life that was out of beer.

We were on the 1100 block of Grace Street, where all the parties happen and the thick summer nights smell like dog shit turning to mud. I'd been coming to parties on this block for years, and had been foolish enough to think that tonight would be different. My newfound blackness didn't come with a guidebook, so I was stuck retreading my old steps and waiting for something new to present itself. Something had, but not in a way I'd expected. What had happened at that show?

Then I heard it coming over the wood fence: hot guitars and knocking drums, Andre 3000's back-of-the-throat voice chanting, "Don't everybody like the smell of gasoline? Well burn, motherfucker, burn American dream."

Outkast never failed to get me excited, but this time, I was elated. I could feel the funk taking the slump out of my shoulders. I could see the soul, a shaft of heavenly purple-hued light beaming into the yard from next door. There was a better party, where they were listening to black music and therefore more likely to actually be black. And it was going down thirty feet away, fifty feet from the blown-out boombox playing heavy metal in the living room of the party where I'd been suffering. I go out to dance and meet people. You don't do that to music that sounds like dangerous construction equipment.

I got on my toes and steadied myself on the damp fence, but still couldn't see into the next yard over. Above the yard was a second-floor balcony with a grimy glass door sitting open, a lamp on inside, and hip-hop pumping out. I could hear a blanket of voices, too, blending into a chatter that didn't sound particularly black or white. They could have been from either party.

I turned from the fence, wiped the slimy wood residue on my shorts, and checked out the party I was already at. There were sad sprouts of grass, cliques of young punks stooped over the last cans of beer, and a tinny singer shouting like a breakup at last call. There was no way that the other party was worse than this. Bravado surged. This was what I'd been waiting for.

"This party's over," I said. "I'm gonna go next door."

The girls looked at each other and nodded. The young drunk guy put his hands on top of the fence to hop it. The rotten wood wobbled. I tapped his shoulder. "If y'all are coming, then we can just walk around."

"Burn, motherfucker, burn American dream" looped in my head as I led a conga line through the brick gangway and onto the seedy block, then up the steps of the next apartment building. At the top, the smudged glass door was propped open by a sodden newspaper. The lobby's musty smell evoked Mona's apartment a block or a world away. A line of corrugated metal mailboxes hung loose on the wall, and the taste of old beer begged to be obliterated by the taste of new beer. What type of cheap beer do black people drink at parties?

The back end of the song beckoned from a flight up. We charged toward the cracked-open door, imagining a boiler room of music waiting inside. I paused on the landing. This was the last moment before my life changed, before I went to good parties as a black man who listened to black music, hopefully with black people. I took a deep breath as if I were about to dive and smelled sweet, fruity smoke.

The girl with the big eyes threw the door open. The four of us tumbled into the living room then stopped in the middle of an empty wood floor, where the disco ball would have been if it was a school dance. Rap music blasted from speakers sitting on a circular table by the balcony door.

Three people sat at the table: a ratty-faced white boy with a pubescent beard and a tie-dyed T-shirt; a black girl with a small 'fro puffing out from under a train conductor's cap; and a heavy-lidded white guy with center-parted hair whose mouth was puckered around a shiny green hose. He popped the hose out of his mouth, sat back, and exhaled. As the smoker's face spread into a lazy grin, I recognized my former coworker Ethan aka Nesta.

The song ended and the interlude started where the woman is moaning, "I'm cool . . . I'm cool . . ."

Nesta spread his arms and shouted, "Welcome!"

The young guy I was with shouted, "Welcome!" back to him.

The woman with the big eyes tried to open the front door to leave. It hit my heel, so I stepped in, shouting, "Oh, hey! Ethan, what's up . . . Nesta? My bad. We were looking for a party. We must have the—"

"Dude, this *is* the party," Nesta shouted. He gestured at his friends. They held green hoses, too, which snaked back to an ornate, three-foot-tall hookah, sitting like a shadeless lamp in between the speakers. The drums of the next song kicked in and I couldn't help but nod, even as I remembered hearing it for the first time with him a few months before.

"I'm Nesta," he announced to his new guests, like he'd just arrived at this conclusion. He pointed at himself, then around the table, doing the slow shout that people do over loud music, or to distant idiots. "This is my girlfriend, Gabrielle, and that's John."

The rat-faced guy waved while taking a drag off the hookah.

"Cool. I'm—" The doorknob slammed the wall behind me and I turned to see the girls filing out, followed by the young guy. I said, "I'm sorry we butted in."

Gabrielle turned down the music to a pleasant thump. I was glad when she didn't remind me of Mona.

"It's cool," Nesta said. "How're things at the coffee shop?"

I shrugged. "Weird, but . . . you know."

"Yeah, I do." He laughed in a condescending way. Nesta had

acted like he was really moving up in the world by taking a job at the ice cream place.

"How's the new job?" I asked.

"B and G's is dank, man." He grooved in his seat and drooped his eyelids. "Come by sometime. I'll hook you up with a scoop."

"Thanks," I said, and didn't bother telling him I'm lactose intolerant.

"Or maybe I'll see you at the college sometime," he continued. "I've been hanging out by the library with this." He pointed a thumb at the hookah right as John shrouded it in smoke. "It's how I met Gabrielle."

Suddenly, I couldn't move. "You're the Hookah Guy?"

Nesta looked proud. "Yeah!" Then paused. "How'd you hear about me?"

"Oh, uh . . ."

Gabrielle made eye contact and my heart fluttered because she was pretty.

"My roommate said he saw someone smoking a hookah by the college library," I said. "That's all."

"Cool." Nesta grinned. "Well, I've always got an extra hose. Hey, what happened to your face?"

I ran downstairs, giggling. But then I burst out into the sticky hot night, where things were just getting started on a block where I was almost too old to be partying, where people seemed to know more about my own life than I did, and things didn't seem so funny.

**EIGHT** I woke up to one of those summer days where you start sweating in the shower and it's impossible to stop. Towel around my waist, I put the needle down on my favorite James Brown song, "Talkin' Loud and Sayin' Nothing."

As the groove kicked in, I picked up the album cover, then dropped it in surprise. Usually, the cover's got a portrait of James in a dark denim bell-bottom suit, sitting on a filthy concrete bench, with his name and *In the Jungle Groove* scrawled on the wall behind him.

I picked it up from the living room floor and carried it into my room. Today, James had company. Across from him, 'fro blocking half the record title, stood a guy who looked just like Lucius. He was wearing a 1970s basketball referee uniform—black pants and a gray V-neck with black piping—and blowing a whistle at James. Alone, James looked satisfied. With the ref in his face, he looked tired and a little defiant, fixing his mouth to go, "Really, you want more?"

The song blared in the living room, muffled a bit by the wall. I love how the shuffling rhythm pushes and pulls at the same time, all headed in the same direction: forward. I propped the record cover up on my dresser and pulled on a black T-shirt and the dirty jeans I'd dedicated to work that week.

When I looked at the record cover again, James Brown was still frozen in place, but the ref had turned and was pointing out beyond the photographer, like he was surprised by something over my shoulder. I turned around. There was Lucius, standing in my bedroom door in a baggier version of my outfit, with white gym socks glowing on his feet.

"Been a minute," we both said, having a standoff in my musty little bedroom.

"Taught you well," he said.

He sure hadn't been doing much teaching lately, but everything felt like a test. So I said, "Where you been? Coulda pulled that cop off me on Russell's porch."

He said, "If I jumped in, things woulda got a lot more serious."

I pointed at my face. "It got pretty fucking serious, Lucius." I turned and rifled around in my dresser for some socks of my own. "That's awful convenient for you. That might be something that'll lose you *your* Black Card," I said.

I turned, holding some socks that were losing their elastic. James Brown grunted and shouted in the empty living room while Lucius stood there making O shapes with his lips like a hungry fish.

Finally, he said, "I never had one, man."

"What?" I looked up, while bent over to put on a sock.

"Dawg," he said, and laughed kinda nervously. "I made that thing on a copy machine back in the day. To chill you out."

"What?" I said again, and stood up straight with one sock on, my bare foot gathering dirt from the splintery floorboards.

"Yup." He nodded. "You should have heard yourself back then. Asking me a million questions."

He sat on the foot of my bed and dropped his voice to sound like mine. "'Why do black people go to church? Why can't my shoes get dirty? Can you show me the Tootsie Roll dance? What are the projects like, do you know?'"

I rolled my eyes and laughed at the embrrassing memories.

I put on my other sock and he said, "Aye, remember when you couldn't understand nobody and we had to work backwards? You thought 'shorty' was 'shad.' 'Lucius, what's "shad"?'"

I laughed. "I still don't get that one. I heard someone call his six-foot-five homie Shorty."

"Hey," he said. "Sometimes you've just gotta use it your own way. Make it work."

"That's what I've been trying to do," I said.

James transitioned into the next song, kicking it off with the usual call-and-response with his band.

"I can tell," he said. "And I'm here to help. Say, you about ready for work?"

"Yeah," I said. "Let's go."

We put on matching dark shades, and the apartment swam in a deep bottle-green murk.

Outside, I turned from locking the front door and Lucius was bending my Black Card with his thumb and forefinger.

I jumped over to grab it. "Gimme that."

The card looked janky and faded in the daylight. Standing on the porch, I turned it over and reread the black privileges on the back. Some of them made sense, like maintaining a healthy skepticism of white folks, and use of the n-word. But some of it seemed silly, like the stuff about flip-flops and socks.

I'd got what I'd been trying to get, but it wasn't what I thought I'd wanted.

"Being black isn't a club," I told Lucius. "There are no ins and outs."

He nodded, divided diagonally by the sun shining under the porch roof. "We're all in, all the time," he said. "You don't really need black lessons from me. The world's a goddamn black lesson."

He sent a nod out toward the coffee shop.

This shift was gonna be with Mona, and I knew that if I took my usual route through the alley, I'd think of every stupid, mean thing I'd said to her until I was even more awkward by the time I arrived. I walked past Lucius and onto the tan sidewalk, taking a right toward Carytown.

"So, what do I do now?" I asked. "There're no Black Cards, so what am I working toward?"

"Being the you that you want to be. So, I say do what you been doing," he said. "Like when you said your piece to that boy from North Carolina the other day."

"Thanks," I said, then winced, remembering JJ's confusion at my blackness. "You think it changed anything?"

"More than if you ain't said nothing," said Lucius. "But . . . for the time you spend converting a single redneck, five more are born."

I pictured a field with endless rows of low plants, cabbage-size white heads popping up from the ground, with mesh-back hats, mullets, buzz cuts, and teased bangs appearing in little clouds of dry dirt.

We stopped at the corner of Ellwood Avenue. A tree waved overhead while a few cars passed, stirring up a wave of hot air. A silver SUV stopped at the curb in front of us. The window oozed down and I saw a middle-aged white man at the wheel, opening his mouth to say something. I kept my mouth shut because you don't provoke a stranger in a big vehicle when you're on foot. After a moment, he squinched his eyes into his sunglasses, then popped his mouth shut and looked forward. The window slid back up and the car rolled off.

"What was that about?" I asked Lucius.

"Oh, you'll see."

We crossed the street. The houses looked the same. So did the cars disappearing down the avenue.

"Lucius, I expected it to feel different," I said.

"What?" he asked

"Being black," I said. "The sun's still hot and I still want another cup of coffee."

"You always been black. Why would that feel different now?" he asked. "White people want you to think it feels different, because they think it would. That's how they justify treating us worse."

"Hell no," I said.

"Mmm-hmm," he agreed. "You're you. Only thing that should feel different is that you're always kinda mad."

I looked around, at the chocolate shop and the deli. That was why this world always seemed like it hadn't been created for me.

"Why didn't you tell me this a few years ago?" I asked. "Coulda saved me some grief."

"You needed to figure it out for yourself," Lucius said. "You weren't there yet. We weren't talking like this back then."

We came up on the parking garage behind the movie theater. Lucius's voice rippled through the concrete structure when he said, "Hey, let me hold your card?"

I hesitated for half a second, then handed it to him, feeling trusting. He stepped to the parking garage entrance and fed my Black Card into the ticket machine. The barricade lifted and Lucius walked in, waving me along over his shoulder as he faded into the darkness.

Inside, the parking garage looked like none I'd ever seen. Instead of cars and parking spaces, a velvet rope ran along the wall, draping lavishly between brass posts. Small spotlights shined up on the framed posters lining the wall. Black faces looked out from each one, smiling, glowering, or holding a pizza box and staring in front of different colored backgrounds, advertising movies I'd seen, and others I made a mental note to check out.

Our footprints were quiet, and I looked down to see that I was walking on wall-to-wall maroon carpet. There was a perfect air-conditioned chill. I caught the toasty, salty, unmistakable popcorn smell and saw a machine in the corner, with nuclear yellow kernels piled up against the greasy glass. Lucius cut a right and I followed him up a ramp with more velvet rope and posters.

Lucius disappeared onto the flat second level while I still climbed. As soon as he was gone from my sight, Blaxploitation conga drums rolled, and some brassy funk with chicken-scratch guitar started to play, piped in through fabric-covered hi-fi speakers mounted along the wall every few posters.

I finished the walk up, Lucius reappearing a foot at a time as I took the last few steps onto level two. He sat facing me in a black beret, legs crossed in a black canvas director's chair. He pointed to the empty, identical chair next to him with a black megaphone, revealing the green-and-red fist painted on its side. A mechanical rumble quivered through the cement beneath the carpet, and when I sat, I saw that a movie screen had scrolled down behind me, blocking the top of the ramp.

I took off my shades and tucked them onto the neck of my shirt as the light dimmed even more. Film clattered into a projector above our heads, and a familiar 4-3-2-1 countdown flickered on the screen in front of us.

The first thing we saw was from a black-and-white movie. Corny old jazz tooted through the speakers as an older black man in a tux and a toothy grin tap-danced down half a flight of stairs and bowed in front of a little white girl. The grin stayed frozen on his face as he took the girl's hand in his gloved fingers and they turned to dance together up the stairs, her imitating his every move as they climbed.

The dancing was impressive, but I couldn't stop thinking how everything hung on that little girl's whims. She could have pushed the man down the stairs, and he wouldn't be able to do anything but keep forcing that skeleton grin.

The screen flashed white, then some color footage of a black woman in a big fuchsia 1980s suit with curlicue accents and matching hat appeared on the screen, dangling a small leather purse from a white-gloved hand. The second character with gloves, because we aren't allowed to touch the white world with our bare hands.

"Our?" Lucius read my thoughts.

"Yup," I said.

Us.

Out of the corner of my eye, I saw him smile and nod.

On the screen, the 1980s black woman stepped back gingerly as a white couple began a dramatic kiss. An oldies ballad hit a crescendo. Seeing the climax of a movie without seeing anything else felt pointless. I had to be at work. I turned to Lucius, my chair's canvas back stretching under my weight.

"Why're we watching movies?" I asked.

He snapped his fingers and the projection stopped.

"I take it you've never heard of a Magical Negro," he said.

"No . . ." I could use one of those. I could be one of those. "Wait," I said. "Is this some more nonsense you made up?"

"I ain't made this up," Lucius said. "It's some nonsense, though."

"So what is it?" I asked, losing my sense of depth as I stared into the hanging silver-white screen.

"It's in a movie or a TV show," Lucius said. "Where there's a black character, and the only reason they're on is to help the white folks. Maybe they're a cool old man with some sage advice. Sometimes they actually have some mystical ability and can make white people good at sports or dancing." He pointed the megaphone at the screen and the tap dancer soft-shoed across it, in sharp relief to the blank background.

"But in movies," Lucius said, "they disappear when their work is done."

"Like a god in the machine, where they come out of the blue to change things?" I asked.

"Yeah," he said. "But I guess they come out of the white."

We both laughed, then I stirred in my chair and said, "I need to get to work."

He waved me back into my seat, "Not yet. We're on Colored People Time in here, the clock's moving differently."

"What about out there?" I asked, pointing toward an exit sign with a cardboard cutout of a woman with a leather jacket, 'fro and pistol standing by it.

"We're on their time out there," Lucius said. "But a Magical Negro's work is never done. We don't disappear."

"We?" I asked.

"What do you think I am?"

I just kinda stared at him as he shrugged. I'd always known that people couldn't see Lucius, but we'd never talked about it, because I didn't want him to go away.

"A'ight." Lucius stood. "Let's go. I think you're gonna see things differently from now on."

We rounded the corner onto Cary Street, shades back on, and I heard weeping as we passed under the century-old Byrd Theatre's ornate marquee. A slim brother with short dreadlocks was sitting in the passenger seat of an SUV, hiding his face with his hands, massaging his forehead with his fingertips, and sobbing loudly.

"Damn, Lucius. Should we check on this guy?" I asked.

"Naw, look." He pointed.

A preppy middle-aged black man in a chino baseball cap and tucked-in polo was climbing out of the driver's seat, paunch first. He was clutching a brown bag from the local conservative Christian grocery chain and making a sour face. The two men didn't match.

"What's going on?" I muttered to Lucius. "They a couple? Or is the older guy his dad?"

"Not quite," said Lucius. "I think that young brotha's worn out from a tough job."

I stopped in front of the vintage store next door and watched the drama. Sobs echoed under the movie marquee, but no one else was looking at the young man crying in the car's front seat. Lucius sidled up to me. A mannequin in a beaded 1920s flapper dress loomed over him from the store window.

It was the beginning of lunch hour, and the sidewalks were busy with men in rumpled suits and women in wilted blouses, dragging themselves along, holding white paper bags and plastic-topped soda cups. Peppered throughout were black people, often walking in pairs, rarely both in professional dress. A punky white bike courier I sorta knew pedaled by, giving me a nod. I wondered if he'd seen Paper Fire with a different bassist.

The preppy black guy shoved his grocery bag into the back of his SUV then slammed the door, and the crying got quiet. A teenage couple were coming toward us, both black kids, both holding colorful ice cream cones. The girl's eyes slid my way before she focused her attention back on her bright green ice cream.

"Walk with me," Lucius said.

We stepped out and I almost bumped into a twenty-something couple who were walking a few feet behind the teen-agers, holding their own ice cream.

I said, "'Scuse me" and stepped aside, then looked closer.

The guy was wearing a blue mail-carrier uniform with the hat turned backwards, and the woman with him had long, thick braids under a jazzy applejack hat. They looked just like char-acters from a black romance movie I'd seen in high school. I watched them until the guy looked my way. I got worried I was gonna get grief for staring, but he nodded. I smiled. Straight up, this was already twice as many black people as I was used to seeing in Carytown. I loved it.

A block later, I looked across the narrow street and saw the dashiki-wearing, gray-dreadlock-having Afrocentric professor guy who comes into the coffee shop for hummus padding down the sidewalk in sandals. He was trailed by a militant-looking brother who was defying summer in a black leather jacket and beret, marching with a rifle on his shoulder.

Once my instinct to duck behind a mailbox passed, I started to think how no black person could get away with carrying a rifle on the street. So what was going on?

Two professional black women in their thirties were smil-ing as they walked into a Thai restaurant. Two '80s sitcom-mom-looking black women ducked in behind them, before the door could clip their broad-shouldered teal-and-kente-cloth blazers. I continued through the bright day, feeling more and more like myself as I walked the last block to work in peace, my favorite bass line running through my head.

———

Three-Piece Tarik lounged in a wrought-iron chair on the coffee shop patio, slowly rolling his tongue across the front of his top teeth as he replaced his mug on the matching wrought-iron table. Across the table from Tarik stretched a brother who was somehow lounging harder, somehow smoother, wearing linen pants that were somehow flowier, and black shades that were somehow darker, setting down a cup that somehow seemed more delicate than Tarik's.

I didn't think that anyone could seem cooler than Tarik, and the surprised laugh that bubbled up inside me added a little soul to my nod when we said hello. Without thinking, I led with my chin, not my forehead.

Tarik's companion's nod was so slow it looked like he was taking a deep breath of mountain air. Tarik saw me watching and nodded too.

I was in on something.

Lucius clapped my shoulder, said, "I'm there for you, brotha, but I'll be out here right now," then tapped his heart with the top of his fist and pulled out a chair to join them.

Who will be with Mona? I wondered, as I tied on an apron in the employee bathroom. Maybe she's got a super-earthy sista guiding her, or she could wish she was hood. I tried to picture Mona in a parka and big gold earrings.

Then I stepped out, smoothing my apron with my palms, and got my answer. She looked an awful lot like Mona, but a few years older, and dressed in a gray wool skirt suit with her locks pulled back into a bun. She could have been Mona's yuppie older sister.

Some neo-soul was on the stereo, a slower song with a synthetic-sounding acoustic guitar. Mona's companion poured steamed milk from a small silver pitcher into a go cup and handed it to regular Mona, who rung up Soy Latte. I smiled at the customer, then said hi to the Monas. The white customer squinted at the espresso machine, trying to figure out why I was talking to it.

Mona said, "Hi."

We worked through the lunch rush. The Monas stayed up front, plunging the metal scoop into the ice machine for cold drinks and bringing food orders back to my kitchen stronghold. During lulls, I'd bus tables, passing between them like an extra point, the smell of their coconut shampoo wafting around me in stereo. It hit me that just by doing it—cutting a sandwich, scraping dried mustard from a plate—whatever I did was undoubtedly black.

Things quieted down by 1:30. I joined the Mona I knew at the counter, with a mental list of things to sincerely apologize for, from the dumb questions I asked at her house, to getting mad at her about the cops, to something I couldn't quite put in words, about how I'd come in too hot and assumed too much.

Before I could start, she said, "They found the guy."

"Oh, shit."

"Yeah," she said.

"Did you have to pick him out of a lineup or something?" I asked. I pictured Mona behind a spotlight, pointing at a row of light-skinned brothers.

"No." Mona stirred her chai tea until there was a tan whirl-pool in the middle. "He was dead."

I wished I'd been the one to kill him, or that Mona could have. But that would have dug the hole deeper.

"What happened?" I asked. "How'd they know it was him?"

"They had a description for a while," she said. "And it fit this guy they wanted for other break-ins," she continued, spitting out that last word. "And they found him in an abandoned house, with a needle near him."

I should have felt relieved, but having some facts made him realer. Finally, really seeing him in my mind made me aware of a distance that had always existed between Mona and me.

"How do you feel?" I asked.

Dead quiet from her, dark eyes gleaming wet. Then, "Still scared."

And I sighed.

"I'm glad you asked, though," she said.

"I should have earlier," I answered.

We let that hang in the air, alongside Mona's airy pop music that I'd never admit to liking.

I started pumping a coffee for myself. The new Mona came out of the kitchen and, without looking at me, bopped Mona's shoulder with her knuckles, sisterly, murmuring, "What else?"

I stood at the airpot, waiting to hear. Mona saw me and I could practically hear her thinking, "You finally figured that out, huh?"

Then Mona said, "I put in my notice. I'm quitting."

The older Mona beamed, leaning by the espresso machine with her hands in her apron pocket.

"Oh," I said.

I was not surprised, but I was sad—because I'd miss her and because I couldn't think of worse circumstances.

"I got an internship up in DC," she explained as her clone smiled behind her. "I'm gonna take a semester off and just . . . do that," she said.

"That sounds perfect," I said.

The less I said, the less chance I'd ruin the calm with my mouth. So we finished our shift quietly, me wondering what came next.

I took the really long way home, and stopped off at the old Vibe Café, where I sat at a dark table by the kitchen and filled out an application, smelling like coffee grounds and all. I didn't recognize anyone. They wouldn't know me. I could do something new there.

The kitchen door swung open and I got a glimpse of a black man in an apron, waving steam off the top of a huge pot. Next to him, a brother in a plaid shorts suit lounged in a beach chair and sipped an electric blue cocktail. Even with them around, working at an Italian spot isn't exactly part of a real-deal brotherman lifestyle. But the tips would be better, and I figured if Mona could want something then go get it, then it might work for me as well.

Plus, each box that I filled in on the application got me thinking that it'd be just about as easy to apply for college, and maybe I should look into that. Not like I had much else to do, or any other idea for how that might change.

_____

It was getting dark and I was walking up Mason's girlfriend's block on my way home when I saw Mason in his royal-blue work polo, placing his guitar case in his car's trunk.

I said, "Aye, Mason."

He turned around, saw me, and quickly slammed the trunk shut, then leaned against it, risking getting dirt on the butt of his black chinos.

I wish we could have just had a laugh about Hookah Guy, but he had some questions to answer. I stopped on the sidewalk.

"Where are you off to with the guitar? We gonna practice?" I asked.

"No," he said.

"OK." I nodded. "You gonna practice with someone else?"

"Uh," he said, and did a nervous laugh. "Russell didn't tell you?" he asked, standing straight and rocking from foot to foot behind his car.

"No . . . ?" The iced coffee I'd drunk while closing up the shop hit my bladder and I started rocking, too.

"Clay's gonna be our new bass player," Mason said.

We stared at each other for a couple of seconds, waiting for a guy in a pro wrestling T-shirt with blue lightning bolts all over it to pass on a rumbling motorcycle. Mason spent the whole time wincing in this condescending way.

"You want me to switch to guitar or something?" I asked, louder than needed, immediately getting embarrassed for sounding so pathetic. I can't play guitar.

"No." Mason sighed and his shoulders dropped.

Oh.

"Clay?" I leaned forward and Mason tensed.

"Yeah. I'm sorry, dude. He can play and you just, you haven't seemed too into it."

"Clay's *into* it?" I asked.

"Yeah," he said.

I thought of the tours we'd talked about going on, the great shows we wanted to have, the classic album we were planning to make.

I sighed. They'd rather do that with Clay than with me.

"I'm sorry, dude." He started bouncing his keys in his hand, like they were just raring to get in his car's ignition.

"I got nothing, man," I said. "I got nothing."

"So did we when you'd get too drunk to play, or skip the whole show," Mason said. "What's that?"

"Me trying not to lose my shit," I said, and stalked off, as if the funk band I really wanted to be in would be waiting on my porch.

It's easy to lose it when you're looking for yourself.

My eyes were starting to tear, so I stared at the sidewalk, which glowed in the dusk. I was too shocked to really be pissed or sad. Mason drove by a minute later and shouted, "I'm sorry, dude," out his window. I flipped him off and saw a streak of brake lights before he gassed it to the stop sign on the next block.

Those tours and albums? They weren't gonna happen anyway.

When I got home, the mailbox was stuffed. I grabbed the letters then walked in. Lucius was asleep on the couch with his head lolling over the back. One of my punk records sat on the cushion next to him. I moved the record back to the stereo then spread the envelopes like a hand of cards. I had one from the City of Richmond, which I split open with my thumb. It was a ticket. Dated July 15. For Public Intoxication. The next sheet was a carbon of intake papers, dated that night and signed by Donahue. They crinkled in my hand, 100 percent real.

For the time being, my city was empty and I was free.

 **NINE** Black guys I am:

Got blamed for something because he's a black guy guy.

Didn't quite crack the code of white secret society guy.

From the south likes southern rap guy.

Likes Tupac a bit more than Biggie because of *Juice* guy.

Gets lost in the bass guitar groove guy.

Run-in with the cops guy.

No car "No Scrubs" guy.

No bike, aspires to be the guy in "No Scrubs" guy.

Likes white music guy.

Has a black imaginary friend because he doesn't have any other black friends guy.

Highwaters tight pants tight shirt guy.

Admits his apartment's a dump guy.

Looks like some other light-skinned guy guy.

Seen for everything he's not guy.

Me guy.

Everything I do guy.

THANK YOU

Kirby Kim, Brenna English-Loeb, and everyone else at Janklow & Nesbit.

Mensah Demary and the rest of the team at Catapult.

Readers Ezra Claytan Daniels, Julia Ingalls, Ashaki Jackson, Joey R. Poole, Aaron Samuels, Cyn Vargas, and Tom Williams.

Members of my novel-writing group, past and present: Cecil Castellucci, Melissa Chadburn, Seth Fischer, Sacha Howells, Meg Howrey, Sarah Langan, Kim Samek, J. Ryan Stradal, and Lenore Zion.

Chicago crew Catherine Eves, Jessie Ann Foley, Samantha Irby, Naomi Huffman, Kevin Kane, and Jacob Knabb.

Eso Won Books, Hot Dish Reading Series, Jack Jones Literary Arts, Kaya Press, Mixed Remixed Festival, Pasadena Literary Alliance, PEN America, *Razorcake* magazine, Writing Workshops Los Angeles, and Writ Large Press for helping me feel at home in Los Angeles.

My family Sharon A. Mooney, Ashley Newton, and the Terrys: Caitlin, Felix, Henry, and Mary.

Extra special thanks to Felix for napping so I could write this thing.

ABOUT THE AUTHOR

Chris L. Terry was born in 1979 to an African American father and an Irish American mother. He spent his teens and early twenties touring the United States and Europe as the singer in different punk bands. Terry has an MA in English from Virginia Commonwealth University and a creative writing MFA from Columbia College Chicago. His debut novel, *Zero Fade*, was named a Best Book of the Year by *Slate* and *Kirkus Reviews*. Terry lives in Los Angeles with his family. He works as a copywriter and creative writing instructor.